A WITNESS TREE

The Story of Hattie Plain

Peter Tyner

Table of Contents

Chapter 1

Blam! The old woman slammed the hall door, but there was no metallic snap. She shoved it with her narrow shoulder, then hit it with her backside. Still no luck. Dropping the Wal-Mart bag, she reared back and rammed it with her cane. *Click.*

All right then. She re-hung the shopping bag on her elbow and made her way down the hallway toward the sunlit foyer. Pausing at the ruined letterbox she raked her mail into the sack, then quickly shuffled outside ahead of the crashing security gate.

An inauspicious start. But Mr. Davis was certainly with her, and the mission was intact.

The morning sky filled with clouds. A breeze kicked up from the East River, bringing the sweet fragrances of fresh apple fritters from Kim's on the Korner near Lennox Park.

Kim's indeed. In 1964 the place was called Trudy's Ribs, known for its sculpture of giant ribs atop two forty-foot poles. If you were hungry and had three dollars in your pocket, you navigated there by the towering sign. If you were lying in Trudy's parking lot bleeding to death, it would have been the last thing you saw.

Duty called. Re-pinning the purple-sequined hat into her gray bun, the old woman tightened her thin blue shawl, and stepped to the rail. From there she easily commanded the vista of 125th Street from Lennox Park to the Zion Redeemer church.

Brownstones lined both sides of the old street, their once bright bricks now darkened with soot and age, their elegant peaked roofs now patchworks of repairs. Clattering busses, cars and trucks weaving through central Harlem filled the morning air with exhaust. But there were visions of another Harlem in her thoughts. Horse-drawn produce wagons chased by packs of squealing children. Stickball in the cobbled street. Waves of arriving colored families.

Closing her eyes, the old woman smiled as once again she mounted the modern red tile steps with the baby and the suitcase, and unflinchingly pressed Bobbi Savoy's bell.

A voice behind the door broke her reverie. "Everything alright, Miss Plain?"

Hattie turned to the building super. "Just fine, Johnny. Just fine." After decades the slight, balding caretaker remained shy as the day he arrived. She nodded toward the overgrown Hickory dominating her small garden. "Say now, you still got that tree trimmer?"

Johnny opened the door and nodded. The branches were now scratching at Hattie's living room window where a sign propped-up behind the glass read, *Rueben Lives.*

Suddenly the staccato reports of nail guns reverberated through the neighborhood. Hattie stood on her toes to see the work site.

"Next block over." The super squinted grimly. "*Re*-development! Comin' here soon enough, I expect." Johnny touched her shoulder before returning to the foyer. "Happy Birthday, Miss Plain."

"Thank you, Johnny." Hattie's smile faded as a black sedan swerved into the parking space in front of her building. A white woman in black slacks and blazer exited the passenger side and studied the walk-ups. A reflective badge dangled from her neck. She glanced repeatedly at a cell phone cupped in one hand.

Police looking for an address. Good luck. Addresses on 125th Street were largely a mystery. Hattie glanced at her own building. The numerals had long since disappeared. But local police would know that. Absorbed by the strangers, Hattie almost didn't notice the passing foot patrol cops. The tall one saluted. "Mornin', Mayor."

The old woman straightened up, nodded slightly and watched them stroll past.

Quickly enough a cab pulled in behind the dark sedan and blared his horn. Hattie recognized him as Jaswant Singh, the math teacher from the seniors center dropping off a fare.

The woman with the cell turned and pointed the badge at him. Unfazed, the cabbie launched a verbal fit from his window. After a moment she surrendered the space, and the cab moved up.

Taking a deep breath, Hattie once more hoisted the Wal-Mart bag. The mission was underway. There was no turning back. Cane first, she began the arduous descent down the dozen broken tile steps. Below her lounged a handful of young men, their pungent tobacco smoke whipped around in the light gust. The tall one looked up as Hattie passed by in her white Nikes a step at a time. He nodded.

"Sup Granny! You lookin' fine today."

"Nothin' to it, Eugene." Hattie shot back. "How's that foot comin' along? You runnin' yet?"

He tried unsuccessfully to shelter the smoke. "No ma'am, but I be good by late summer."

"You keepin' trash out my garden?"

"Yes ma'am."

"All right then." Hattie stepped onto the sidewalk. "Read newspapers if you ain't gonna be in school now, hear?"

"Yes ma'am."

She turned toward the bus stop and shifted her bag. Clouds were rapidly darkening the eastern sky; spring showers would surely come by noon. But there was still plenty of time to get to 42d Street on the Lexington bus. Still time to redeem everything. She had barely taken two steps when the sound of squealing brakes turned her head.

The sedan had returned, this time with a flashing red light in the windshield. A license plate sign read "Official U.S. Government Business." Squinting east against the bright clouds, Hattie watched the man display a badge to Eugene and his friends. The woman with the hanging tag bolted the stairs, rang the doorbell, and stood back.

Hattie picked up the pace. The bus stop was still half a block away.

Chapter 2

"Hattie!" A familiar voice rang out. Arms pumping, Ruth caught up, her tall form slightly bowed. "You didn't hear me yellin' at you from that cab back there? My, that little foreign driver is rude, honey, all looking at my legs while I'm fighting my way out of that back seat. There's no Bible-readin' goin' on in that house, uh-uh."

Ruthie wore long curls whitened with age and clutched a black suede handbag. Puffy bags sat below piercing brown eyes. Horn-rimmed glasses hung from her neck on a beaded strap.

"What is this now, birthday girl?" Ruthie looked her friend over. "Where you going in your Sunday best, on a *Monday?*" She donned the glasses and glanced into the bag. "What you got in that sack anyway?"

Hattie pulled the bag away and began walking. "Out my way Ruth, I got me an important meeting. And that bag is my business."

Ruth easily kept pace with her shorter friend. "You going to the doctor? You getting dizzy again?"

Hattie waved her away. "You got me confused with some old lady."

"Somebody having a birthday party for you then? I see you got your bus pass out. Where's this party gonna be?"

Hattie waved her off again. "Gonna be in heaven if you don't let me be."

Ruth stopped. "Hattie Plain, I been your neighbor and friend forty-five years. What's this about?"

Hattie paused, then pulled a newspaper from the shopping bag and shook it at her. "The Advice columnist at the Daily Record, name of Jamie Workman, Jumpin' Jamie they call her, just left her job, and I aim to replace her."

Ruth's mouth fell open. "The New York Daily Record? Hattie, you just a crazy old . . ."

Hattie's face flushed. "Don't you be going on about how I'm too old. I ain't too old, I got me just enough experience to do that job right."

"What experience?" Ruth dropped her jaw. "Hattie Plain, you ain't worked one day at a newspaper!"

"That ain't the kind of experience I'm talkin' about, Ruthie." Hattie adjusted her rimless spectacles and checked her watch. "Fact is I *did* work in a paper." She turned and commenced the brisk walk.

The two women passed Zion Redeemer Church where a noisy tanker truck was pumping April heating oil into subterranean tanks. The roaring engine almost drowned out pre-recorded church bells marking the nine o'clock hour. Hattie sniffed. Few people were still around who remembered the building as the Tuxedo Club where Jamal Handler and a hundred other musicians got their start.

"You the *honorary* mayor of 125th Street, honey, it don't count anywhere else." Ruth stayed beside her. "I told you this was a waste of your time last month when you wrote them that letter."

Hattie kept moving. "Letter of introduction, Ruth. It's the professional way."

"But they didn't answer you, did they? That was your first clue, girl. You on a fool's errand."

"Uh huh. And when's the last time somebody just handed you something you really wanted?" Hattie shook her finger. "Ruthie, they need somebody just like me in that job, and you know it."

Ruth's tired face became animated as she leaned closer in. "Hattie, honey, they ain't lookin' for a ninety-two-year old retired janitor to do nothin' except clean their toilets and buy their newspapers." Ruth searched Hattie's face. "Look here now, girl. Birdie baked you a fine birthday cake down at the center. Let's go celebrate and let these people be."

Hattie adjusted her hearing aid and shook the paper at Ruth. "You see this? It says the paper is gettin' a face-lift. Looking for a younger audience, it says. Humph. When's the last time you saw a teenager read a newspaper? Somebody over there done lost their mind."

She took her place in line as the bus groaned to a stop at the nearby red light.

Ruth put an arm around her shoulders and leaned down. "You gonna go down there and make them white business people listen to you? This ain't about the back of the bus honey, this ain't worth whatever it is you're going to have to put yourself through, with your pain-in-the-neck stubbornness."

Hattie fished a note from her purse and handed it to Ruth. "Look here, Ruthie, I want you to call a gentleman at the New York Times if I ain't back by six o'clock tonight. He's the night editor, name of Benson Ridges. This here's his direct number. Tell him what you know. You got that?"

Ruth looked at the note and flapped her arms. "What you want me to say to this man Benson Ridges, crazy woman? My friend Hattie who cleaned the bathrooms in your building for sixty-one years is now looking to be the Advice Columnist for your competition and she ain't back from the interview yet?"

Ruth stared down a small group of eavesdroppers, then lowered her voice.

"Or Hattie Plain is in jail again? Mercy, Hattie, here I am eighty-four years old, and you puttin' me back into your game?"

The oncoming bus squealed to a stop and the door hissed open. The line began moving. Hattie took Ruth by her shoulders and peered up into her eyes. "You just too young to understand. Do what I ask, Ruth. Be my reliable friend on this."

Hattie found a seat behind the driver and momentarily the vehicle lurched into traffic. She reached into the bag and pulled out a piece of mail from her letterbox. It was a birthday card from the publisher of the *East Hattiesburg Caller.* Under the logo were the words "Over One-Hundred

Forty Years of the African-American Voice." Inside a single, unfolded card bore a few lines of newspaper type.

Help Wanted: Woman of color and hope. Ninety plus years exp. Bring love. Ralph Benjamin Waters, publisher.

Hattie smiled. Every year he had a different way of saying the same thing. Then she noticed a second envelope stuffed inside the first one. She shook out a CD and held it up. The cover had a picture of a white girl in a cowboy hat with a guitar. Her leg was propped on the bleached skull of a cow. The title read:

Michele Banks:
Live at the Opry
Love is Always New

There was a note.

> *Miss Plain,*
>
> *I think of you always, but particularly these days as I go over forty. Careers don't last forever except maybe in your case. I use my voice in Nashville, but I found it in Hattiesburg. Thank you.*
>
> *In case you're wondering, things didn't go well with Cotton. I wound up with an abortion. I wrote it all out in a suicide note, but then re-read it every day for a week, like you told me to do. And I prayed. The 'importance' thing took care of itself. Thank you again and God Bless You. Michele Banks*

Hattie left the rest of the mail in the sack. Gathering her purse and package under her folded arms, she slumped back. It had been a long journey. Ruth was right about one thing; it wasn't about the back of the bus anymore. Her hand rested on a small lunch she'd packed; string cheese, peanut butter crackers and a Diet Coke. She closed her eyes for the half-hour trip to 42d Street and 8th Avenue. Food and rest were essential. No telling how long she'd be at the Daily Record.

Chapter 3

**

August 1930.

Seventeen-year-old Hattie stacked up the dishes in the kitchen sink. Muffled shouting from the yard drew her attention. Drying her hands, she ran to the living room window and looked down into the tiny yard.

"Get out my garden!"

The teenager grabbed her broom and charged on to the stoop. In the cultivated patch, three white youngsters were pummeling a smaller white boy of about twelve.

"Stop it!" Hattie hollered. "Y'all hear me now?"

The surprised boys looked up. The bloodied lad scrambled to his feet, away from the others.

Hattie ran down the steps and immediately straightened the bent Hickory seedling. It wasn't broken, thank God. She confronted the bullies.

"Now, why in the world you trying to kill this boy?"

The stocky, red-faced leader stood his ground. "You're just a monkey so to hell with you."

Hattie swatted the loudmouth over the head with her broom.

"Ow!" He raised his hands to protect himself, but the second blow dropped him to his knees. "That hurts! Stop!"

She turned and glared at the other two bullies, who quickly stepped back. "I run a mop for a living, boys and I can whup you all good. Now who wants to talk this out?"

The disheveled victim straightened out his floral summer shirt. "They hate me for some reason."

The second boy pointed at him and snarled. "You need an ass-whuppin."

Hattie leaned over and kissed the battered boy's forehead. "Nobody hates you, baby, these people just scared of change." She stroked the leaves out of his hair. "Is that what you're going do now, be afraid for the rest of your life?"

"But I didn't do a thing to provoke ..."

"Neither did I, honey." Hattie marched the four boys to the steps and made them sit down. Her smooth, oval face was topped with a wide red bandana, framing saucer-like brown eyes, a button nose and full lips. She examined the victim, a long-faced young man with tight circles of brown hair. Pulling the damp dishrag from her apron, she wiped away the dirt and blood from his wide forehead. She straightened the bent frame of his broken glasses and refit them to his tear-streaked face.

Hattie squinted at the bully. "Now what exactly is your problem with this boy right here?"

"He's an idiot, doesn't belong here, and he's been coming over here to make friends with all them new niggers movin in."

"Well I declare." Hattie shook off the insult. In some ways New York wasn't that different from Hattiesburg. "What's your name, boy?"

"Sean Morrissey." He folded his arms. "And I ain't no boy, I'm twelve."

Hattie spied a group of black children watching from across the street. "You have a problem with your new neighbors, Sean Morrissey?"

"They're takin' over Harlem. My dad says all the white people are gonna get pushed into the East River. Idiots like this kid just let it happen." He tried spitting at the roughed-up boy, but his mouth was too dry. "My dad says us Irish have to fight back."

Hattie dusted off the victim's cap and handed it to him. She noticed the bat from the stickball game lying by the sidewalk. "Don't you think you should wait until you've played some stickball with these new folks before you judge them?"

The bully scorned his victim. "Them kind can't play stickball."

"No?" She turned to the trembling boy. "And what's your name son?"

There was no reply.

"You don't have to be afraid of sayin' your name."

Morrissey sneered. "His name is Ben. Ben the idiot."

"Ben. That's a good name. Is it short for Benjamin?"

The loud-mouth shot back. "It's short for Ben the idiot."

As they spoke a LaSalle automobile pulled alongside the curb. The chauffeur jumped out and hurried over to the little group. "What has happened here?" He glared at Hattie. "Did you allow these hoodlums to attack this boy?"

Sean Morrissey scurried a few yards away with his friends.

"Yeah she made us beat him up cause he's a fairy."

Ben ran to the car and watched from behind the window. Hattie contemplated the LaSalle and the outraged chauffeur. "The boy likes to mingle with whites and Negroes. That against the law in your world?"

"Our world is none of your business." The driver looked at Hattie's building, then up and down the neighborhood. "You'll not be seeing him again."

Chapter 4

**

Hattie emerged from the elevator, and cautiously made her way across the shiny marble floor to the directory marquee. Behind her the automatic doors rumbled shut. The stone floors and deep walnut panels seemed to amplify the sounds of her shuffling footsteps.

It took a moment to realize the annoying musical sounds he was hearing were ringing phones and the pinging of arriving and departing elevators. It reminded her of the casino she'd visited last year when the Seniors Center got a free bus ride.

Free, she scoffed, remembering Ruthie's bitter tears over a vanished Social Security check. Nothing free about it.

Out of nowhere a public address system paged the name Mallory.

Hattie stopped at the unmanned glass reception desk and looked around. Above her, an array of ceiling lights softly illuminated the polished room. The backlit emblem on the wall caught her attention. It glowed,

The New York Daily Record
Founded 1938
Independent and Accurate.

A chic brunette in a striped business suit clacked across the floor toward her, her ample chest and shiny short hair bouncing in rhythm. Bangles swung from both ears as she flashed a brief smile and moved toward the house telephone. The scent of perfume was strong. Noticing the out-of-place visitor, she paused. "Well hello there. I'm Mallory, corporate communications, can I help you?"

Hattie drew herself up. "I'm Hattie Plain, I'm here to be considered for the job of Advice Columnist."

"I see." Mallory looked Hattie over, and smiled. "Actually Ms. Plain, we're not looking to fill that position right away."

"Mm-hm." Hattie scanned the suite. The reception area opened onto a larger room where a gold leaf sign read, *Administration.* The first set of cubicles was labeled *Human Resources.* Other panels read *Security* and *Information Technology.* A trio of cushioned chairs was strung along the wall near the drinking fountain. Hattie set her bag down on the floor.

"I wrote you a letter two weeks ago on the subject but nobody wrote back."

Mallory nodded slightly. "Well, there are changes going on at every level, Miss Plain. We'll answer all our mail when there are answers to give and people to give them. Okay?"

Mallory turned to answer a ringing phone.

"Meanwhile," she chirped, "the floors are quite slick so careful on your way out!" She paused for Hattie to leave. "And thanks for thinking of us!"

Hattie glanced at the elevator doors, then back to Mallory, whose telephone voice had a distinct edge and carried easily.

"I'm in the lobby now, Lonnie. A minor delay. On my way."

Hattie stepped up. "Minor delay?" Mallory lowered the phone. "Excuse me?"

Hattie controlled her outrage. "Girl, I've read every newspaper you've printed for sixty-seven years. *Mother Grace,* remember that column? And *Sadie Says!* That was basic training for me. Then *Jamie's Jumpin'!* Advice that meant somethin'! Look here, I can help others, same way."

The administrator narrowed her eyes. "I'm sure you can, dear. And no, I don't remember sixty-seven years ago. But as I told you, there's no opening. Let's get clear on that! *No opening.*" She turned and strode away. "Bye bye now."

Hattie called after her. "Jamie Workman, she was fired though, right?

Mallory slowly turned. "She is no longer employed here, Miss Plain. That's all I'm going to say."

Hattie was energized. "Alright then, the job is open! Talk to *me* about it."

The thirty-ish clotheshorse seemed amused. "You know, Miss Plain, I think we're all done with that issue, and I'm a bit jammed right now, so if there's nothing else, good day. Again."

"Oh, you jammed alright." Hattie picked up the shopping bag and followed her as far as the visitors' chairs. She held the bag like a baby, adjusted her glasses, and stared at the Human Resources sign. "Anybody in there?"

"That's Mr. Humphries' office. He's Personnel Manager, and he'll tell you the same thing."

Hattie sat down, planting the bag in her lap, and began humming with closed eyes.

"Oh, I see." Mallory folded her arms. "You're tired. How about some water before you go?"

"Look at me, sister." Hattie Plain locked eyes with Mallory. "If by some miracle you survive as long as me, you'll get stronger. Now, stronger ain't necessarily meaner but it does involve a certain amount of conviction."

Hattie gestured at the shopping bag. "Look here, I came all this way to share my resume and to discuss how I can properly bring my unique experience to bear on the job of Advice Columnist. So, don't try and move me back onto the bus, sister, and don't you dare tell me I can't straighten things out for the confused hearts and broken souls who still rely on your newspaper."

The younger woman marched to the HR sign and snapped a piece of paper off the cubicle wall. She spun around and thrust it toward Hattie.

"As you can see by this written and posted policy, employment interviews take place between eight-thirty and noon on even numbered Tuesdays. You'll need to pre-apply on-line, and you'll receive an appointment by email if we're interested. Is that better? I'm so sorry for your inconvenience. May I now assist you to the elevator?"

"I'll tell you what you can do." Hattie handed the document back. "You can bring me the editor of the Advice department." Hattie banged her cane. "Now!"

Mallory backed away with an oath, then turned and disappeared into the labyrinth of cubicles.

Hattie dug through her bag and selected an album page protecting a yellowed newspaper column. Smiling, she held it in better light.

February 1, 1938

Dear Mother Grace, nobody should regret a misspent life as much as I do. I won't face another day of it. I have no excuse; I made wrong choices just because I could. Now I have a skin disease. My hair is falling out. My parents won't talk to me. I'm not welcome in their home. I feel the Lord needs to take me back and re-issue me with a new soul. But the truth is I don't want another chance. I want to disappear. Let me give this warning to your readers; you can "entertain angels unawares," or you can dance with the devil and hobble into the night like me.

Regret

Dear Regret,

*If you're still around to read this, <u>shame
on you</u> for wanting to take the easy way out;
for bringing dishonor on your parents; and for
what you're about to do to those people who find
your body and have to deal with it. Shame on
you for acting helpless. You think it's too late?
You'll find out you're wrong on that too. Go do
something good for somebody today and quit
pitying yourself.*

Mother Grace

Hattie looked up to see a balding man with glasses
standing in the mouth of the HR cubicle. The nameplate on
the cushioned wall read Maurice Humphries. He would no
doubt be the manager, the one mentioned by Mallory.

Humphries looked around, and then spoke to the
communications executive standing in the door to his
office.

"I don't see anybody."

Mallory joined him and pointed at Hattie. He removed
his glasses and cleaned them with his tie.

"Her? Must be some mistake. That old woman's a
retired swing shift janitor at the Times. I used to see her
when I worked nights as a student intern. A million years
ago." He came a step closer.

"Are you the one looking for a job? Here?"

Hattie slipped the old newspaper column back into her bag and stood, offering her hand.

"My name is Hattie Plain."

Humphries stayed back.

Hattie's smile faded. "What is your name, sir?"

"That's not important," he intoned. "I am the personnel manager here and you need to understand what our policies are and respect them. Please leave now."

Hattie sat down again. "Well I don't deal with no-names. And I ain't leavin' till somebody at this newspaper starts takin' me seriously."

Chapter 5

**

April 1926.

Miriam Jones sat face-to-face with the old editor on her birthday. "I'm thirteen now, Mr. Davis. I've been writing essays and obituaries for this newspaper almost a year, now." She drew herself up in the wooden chair and raised her chin. "I hope you agree that I'm ready for promotion to reporter for the Caller."

Davis knitted his brow.

"You know I haven't run much of anything you've turned in Miriam. Not that it isn't good enough…" He scraped the bowl of his cold pipe into a wastebasket and repacked it from a foil tobacco pouch. "Fact is, your essays and observations reveal a certain hope unusual in this part of Hattiesburg. Some may even call it naiveté."

Miriam sat still. Mr. Davis always used the finer language and she enjoyed listening. "Yes sir."

"And, your wise use of simple language would certainly endear you to the hearts of my readers." Davis squinted at the girl above the gold-rimmed glasses. "But you're young. These folks haven't heard a young voice yet."

"Yes sir …"

"And what would your parents do without you helping out at home, you being the only child?"

Miriam jumped up. "My parents want me to break free of the mill!" She waxed excited. "Oh Mr. Davis, understand now, I read the New York Times every single day, I surely do. And the Caller too, every issue. I'll do everything, write essays and report the news and clean those rollers and set the type, as long as there's hours in a day I'll work!"

The girl watched as Davis surveyed the cramped two-room shop. There was the hand-operated printing press taking a third of the back room. Next to it the squat wood cabinet bore trays stacked with leaden characters. Bales of newsprint filled one corner; metal containers full of inks and solvents leaned against the brick wall.

The old publisher's office also left little space to navigate. Unopened mail overflowed the in-basket. The layout for tomorrow's edition spread half completed across a worktable. Ponce sat back and fired up his pipe, well away from the combustible ink solvents whose strong odors permeated the office and the pressroom. A sweet fragrance of cherry-laced tobacco settled in the air.

"Miriam, we're growing and I'm becoming an old man. You want to carry on here some day?"

The girl nodded vigorously. "I do."

Mr. Davis held up two fingers. "Then there are two things I want you to do first. Finish your secondary schooling with top grades. "A"s in English, hear?"

Miriam smiled. Schoolwork came easy for her. "Yes sir."

"And second," Davis scanned the crowded suite, "plan on working here an hour before and two hours after school, three days a week Monday, Wednesday and Friday. You'll clean up, set type and ink up those rollers in the afternoon, then break down the type, and clean the rollers in the mornings. Open mail and organize my desk. I'll pay you twenty cents a day. Do all that and we'll talk about a fulltime reporting job."

Miriam sat forward. "Can I continue writing my Essays on Life?"

The question hung in the air. Ponce Davis arose and went to the bright window looking onto Mobile Street.

"Mr. Davis." Miriam stood and turned. "My Uncle Malcom says my free-spirited voice could prove harmful to your newspaper. Do you think that's true?"

Davis stood silently at the window.

Miriam could see the object of his interest, a panel truck parking out front. Out stepped two men. She recognized the one as Hiram Briggs, Negro bank owner, and the other man with blueprints under his arm as Samuel Boudreaux, site superintendent. She already knew about the imminent construction of a new Mobile Street High School for negroes, an issue for which Mr. Davis had campaigned in editorials for years. Although the source of funds for the project was not completely identified yet, the black community would at last have its own school. And she'd be in that school in its inaugural year.

"Well I know something about voice Miriam." Davis turned. "As you well know I founded the Caller as a handout sheet in the winter of 1865." He nodded, smiling. "I was thirteen years old, your age, a freed slave with big ideas. Most of my audience was illiterate you know. But those of us who could read, why we taught the ones who couldn't. Literacy spread that way." He gestured toward the two men outside the window. "Keeps on going and pretty soon you got your own school."

Hattie suppressed a smile. Mr. Davis rarely spoke to her on such a personal level.

Davis continued. "Well as the ex-slave population grew, this newspaper kept pace too, you know. It's been a sixty-one-year journey from handouts to the hand press." He polished his glasses. "Now the next fifty years is knocking at this old door."

"Yes sir."

He turned to her, his face engraved with the decades-long mission.

"Miriam, hiding your voice to protect you would be the cruelest of all ironies. You're asking me if you can continue Essays on Life?" He smiled at his protégé. "I expect nothing less."

Miriam clasped her hand over her mouth and covered up a joyful scream. "Two dollars and forty cents a month! For doing something I love! When can I start?"

Ponce Davis looked through the crowded calendar. "Well nineteen twenty-six is half gone already." He cleaned his spectacles. "You ask your folks, then come back here and tell me whether they give it the blessing."

Chapter 6

Hattie heard the elevator open and scrutinized the exiting passengers. There was no telling who they might send to talk with her after the confrontation with Humphries and Mallory.

She watched a worker in a brown jumpsuit push a tool cart off the elevator into the lobby. He stopped at the drinking fountain. Graying hair showed under the brown work cap bearing the logo of the Daily Record. The badge dangling from his neck read Facilities Maintenance.

He smiled at her. "And how you doing today, mama?"

Hattie nodded. "What's your name, sir?"

"Everett Washington Junior Ma'am. Sector 2 Maintenance, plumbing and electrical. At your service."

The old woman shifted in the chair.

"I'm Hattie Plain, Mr. Washington. Here for a job interview. But so far I ain't getting anywhere." She sat back. "But you know brother, right things always work out, you give'm enough time."

Washington chuckled. "Enough time, huh? That been my problem?"

Hattie cast a disapproving look. "Why, you look like you doin' fine from here."

"Well I suppose you're right, Miss Plain. Good luck now." Washington moved on.

April 1926

Local Student Joins Editorial Staff

My name is Miriam Jones. My parents are Oswega and Rupert Jones and this is the biggest moment of my life. So far! Mr. Ponce Davis the editor and owner of the East Hattiesburg Caller has asked me to write down my thoughts about life here in East Hattiesburg, Mississippi to be printed from time to time in the feature, Essays on Life.

My subjects are you, my friends and neighbors. Folks around here are quite interesting, good- humored and hard-working; reliable, like hardy trees planted by life's waters. Around here everybody's great-grandparents were slaves. Boll Weevil killed off the cotton, but axe-men say there's no better timber in the world than right here. Now almost everybody works for the lumber mills.

But for some reason the twenty years of prosperity that has swept southern Mississippi didn't reach too far into East Hattiesburg. I've wondered about that, why we don't move forward a little more. It seems folks around here believe

*that tomorrow is just going to be more of today,
stretched out a little thinner.*

*My parents have taught me today's struggle
is nothing but preparation for tomorrow's
miracle. Along the way we become each other's
witness. Spread the word! Talk to your neighbors
by talking to me!*

By two p.m. the lunch crowd had come and gone.
People crisscrossed the lobby, in and out of the elevator,
but no one stopped to talk with the old woman with the
sack, seated by the drinking fountain. Hattie folded her
hands and closed her eyes.

It was nearly three o'clock in the afternoon when she
awoke. The first person she recognized was Humphries
standing by the elevator with two security guards, watching
her.

She ignored them and they soon left. She knew they'd
be back. Hattie pulled more mail from the bag including a
letter bearing the logo of New York City Hall, Department
of Planning, Rehabilitation Division.

Dear Miss Plain,

*The NYC Building Rehabilitation
Department wishes to inform you that apartment
buildings on 125th Street between Lexington
and Lennox Avenue have been approved for
remodel and/or reconstruction in the year 2007.
Displaced residents will receive assistance*

under the Renovation Displacement Assistance
Act, a copy of which is being sent to you under
separate cover.

Well there goes the neighborhood, she thought, amused by her own joke. Johnny was looking like a prophet.

There was more but Hattie folded up the letter and returned it to the bag. It was time for peanut butter crackers. The warm Diet Coke began to fizz out when she tried to open it. Suddenly a hand thrust a paper towel under the soda and lifted it away. It was Everett Washington. He filled a paper cup with cold water from the fountain and presented it.

"What you still doin here, Hattie Plain? You my mother's age and it's killing me to see you sittin' here all day and nobody helping you. But they sure talking about you. Don't you know you ain't got no chance of getting a job here or anywhere else, you too damn old!"

Hattie drank the water and said nothing.

Washington continued his rant. "I'm sixty-two and I ain't gonna be here in six months. They like young! Don't ask me why either, cause I'm their best worker."

"Health insurance goes up as the hair grows gray." Hattie laughed. "It's why I ain't moppin' today, Mr. Washington."

The maintenance man wagged his head. "Nothin' different about this place, Miss Plain. You'd be doin' yourself a good turn by headin' straight out of here and right soon."

Hattie lifted her head. "Well Mr. Everett Washington I don't care two hoots about what you think of my chances of doing anything in this life." She toasted slightly with the Dixie Cup. "But I do thank you for the water."

"Well I'm just trying to save you grief, Miss Plain."

He stepped back and peered down the hallway.

"You sit there now and be stubborn as you want, and I'll be watching Security haul your old black butt outta here in a wheelchair. You ain't exactly in a democracy here."

"Well then, that's good enough, Mr. Washington, cause that'll be the only way I'm leaving without an interview." Hattie waved him away. "Get on with your job sir, don't let me be the cause of your getting fired prematurely."

The maintenance man muttered and, wrangling the loaded cart, disappeared down the hallway.

Hattie opened another piece of mail. It too was a birthday card. She opened it to a hand drawn cartoon depicting a gang of octogenarians waving mops. The text read,

Hattie, you made us proud to be janitors.
Love,
the (remaining) Broadway Mops.

The retired janitor grabbed her cane and chuckled all the way to the ladies room. Upon her return she was surprised to see a new visitor in the next chair.

The middle-aged woman sat perched on the edge of the blue fabric seat with a sheaf of folders in her lap, well-dressed but hardly chic like the Mallory woman. Her coiffed platinum hair framed sad blue eyes and a small, bright red mouth. Her earnest, full face sat above a blue blouse that pulled slightly apart at the buttons. She energetically extended a hand.

"Miss Plain? I'm Elizabeth Whitefield, may I speak with you for a moment?"

"Now that depends, Miss Whitefield." Hattie shook her hand. "What exactly do you do for the paper?"

Whitefield paused. The wily guest had surprised her with a tough question.

"What do I do? I'm Mr. Kendall's administrative assistant."

Hattie nodded. "And who is he?"

Whitefield spoke deliberately. "He's the Features Editor. Crossword puzzle, comics, restaurant and entertainment reviews, letters to the editor… and the Advice column."

"Well, fine then." Hattie faced Whitefield squarely. "Are we going to talk about the Advice job?" She lifted the bag. "I got me a resume right here…"

Elizabeth Whitefield gently stayed the bag with her hand.

"Miss Plain, we're going in a new direction with the features. More along the lines of celebrity gossip, gadgets, fashion, hip-hop culture, a little edgier than what we've been doing the last sixty-seven years."

"Um hmm." Hattie stifled a yawn.

"Mostly it's the vision of our new Managing Editor James Pierce." She shrugged. "Anyway, the lovelorn readership has sadly moved away from us and we need an answer for the new generation." Whitefield dropped her gaze.

"What they got you talking to me for, Miss Whitefield? Don't you know I'm expecting a job interview, not a brush-off?" Hattie took her hand and squeezed it. "Honey, you seem like a fine lady to me, but they gonna have to get past this dumb game if they gonna deal one way or the other with me, you know." Hattie smiled. "They all think I'm too old. That make any sense to you?"

Whitefield let go of Hattie's weathered hand.

"You know, to be honest with you, Ms. Plain, I'm fifty years old myself, and I'm afraid these changes will probably keep us both out of the future."

"Humph!" Hattie stood up to refill her cup at the fountain. "So you're planning to lose all your value? Just one day you gonna stand up and head for the horizon? Umm-um. Not me. I'm just finding my voice, sister. And I've got plenty of it to give."

Whitefield looked around furtively. "Someone has to value your voice enough to pay you."

"They got to hear it first." Hattie sat down again. "So why didn't they value Jamie Workman?"

The blonde spoke softly. "Jamie's voice was, well, a little dated for the audience we're now seeking."

Hattie shook her head. "What world you people livin' in? She had the wisdom of ten people; she was in that job twenty-five years! Then one day she's too old for the room? Mercy. What's she doing with herself?"

"At home I believe." She glanced right and left. "Open to phone calls I hear!"

Hattie scribbled in her notebook, tore out the page and handed it to Whitefield. "You tell her to call this man and explain her situation."

Elizabeth studied the note and looked up slightly confused. "That's a New York Times prefix. Who is Benson?"

Hattie leaned in. "Ain't your business. Just give it to the girl."

Whitefield folded the note and stood.

"Hmmm. You're different, I'll say that much."

"I ain't different honey, I'm real. Maybe around here that's different, I don't know."

Hattie stood with Whitefield. "Now I want to see Mr. Kendall."

Whitefield sighed. It was time to drop the other shoe.

"He's not here, Miss Plain. . . anymore."

"Then who is above him?"

Elizabeth again checked out the room for eavesdroppers.

"The Albrecht family owns the newspaper, and Lonnie Albrecht is the VP of Operations. She's the one who hired Mr. Pierce, the man making all the changes around here." Hattie chuckled. "So which one of them can make the decision to hire me?"

Elizabeth sighed. "If you plan to make an issue out of this, then you'll have to see Mr. Pierce. But watch out, he can be brutal. Actually, they both can."

The old woman touched the Wal-Mart bag.

"Uh huh. I ain't looking for a fight, Miss Whitefield, I'm looking to fill a position that needs somebody like me in it."

Whitefield forced a smile and squeezed Hattie's hand.

"Well I tried to warn you." Whitefield stood up, smoothed the wrinkles from her beige pants and walked away.

Hattie's voice rang clearly down the hall.

"Tell the sister to make that call!"

Hattie relaxed again in the steel chair. She reached for the bag and withdrew a notebook. Leafing through the ancient documents, she paused. Momentarily a smile overtook her sad ancient face.

Chapter 7

Well for three years I've been setting type, inking and cleaning rollers and learning the newspaper business from Mr. Davis. I've also finished my studies with good marks. 'A's in English! Now the time has come. I start work full-time as a Reporter for the Caller tomorrow. To start, I'll be covering the visit of Elois Coleman Patterson to the East Hattiesburg Public Park, tomorrow, Saturday April 14, 1929 to speak on "The Sky's the Limit!", the heroic story of her late sister, aviatrix Bessie Coleman. Miss Coleman, who perished in 1926, was the first licensed female pilot in America, the first woman to obtain an international license, and the first Negro dare-devil air show pilot to perform nation-wide.

The wall clock read Four-thirty. Daily Record employees were now rushing about with parcels, letters and overnights, ignoring the senior citizen with the Wal-Mart bag parked in the chair by the drinking fountain. The pinging elevator doors opened and closed incessantly. Hattie waited. Momentarily a security guard appeared.

"Good afternoon, Madam!" He stood before her and they locked eyes. "I'm Officer Ricky Potente with Security Services. I need you to leave the building immediately." The young man held out an arm. "Permit me to assist you, please."

Hattie sipped her water. "I'm Hattie Plain and I will do exactly that, Officer Potente." The visitor adjusted herself in the seat. "Right after I see Mr. James Pierce."

"Respectfully ma'am, that's not going to happen."

He squatted down to address her. His stocky physique and olive skin contrasted with the white shirt embroidered with his name.

"I'll call a wheel chair up from storage. You'll be comfortable in it all the way out to the street." He paused. "And you will be in it, Ms. Plain."

Hattie slowly stood, gripping the cane mid-staff she drew it back like a baseball bat.

"Get in my way Mr. Potente and I'll put you in that chair."

April 1929
STAY TOGETHER AND PEACEFUL
By Miriam Jones and Ponce Davis

Yesterday April 14. While a hundred residents of East Hattiesburg sat peacefully in the public park listening to a recounting of the heroic deeds of Negro Aviatrix Bessie Coleman, the Klan launched an unprovoked assault with horses and wagons. Many attendees were hurt. Mrs. Sophie McLean was killed under the steel wheels of one wagon bearing the advertising of Ketchum Hardware and Dry Goods.

Sophie McLean is survived by her husband Malcom, of Palmers Crossing. They had no children.

Her nephew, Rupert Jones, attempting to defend his family, inflicted injuries upon J.J. Ketchum, the Proprietor. Jones was arrested. Ketchum was not. These charges will require vigorous defense, the outcome heavily dependent upon the expert counsel of an experienced, politically connected defense attorney. An appeal for donations to acquire the services of such an attorney is underway and money can be dropped off at the offices of this newspaper.

Citizens of East Hattiesburg call upon you Governor, where is the law? And upon you, Lawmakers, where are our guaranteed protections? Long live freedom, life, liberty and the pursuit of happiness!

**

The Security Guard jumped back. "Okay Ma'am. Listen to me now. You can't win this. Just make it easy for both of us, OK?"

He reached out to take Hattie's arm, but she swatted him with her cane. Grimacing, Potente exercised his stricken limb.

A handful of employees slowed down to watch. His subject stood five feet away resolutely holding her cane like a weapon.

"I ran a mop for sixty years sir. Now you behave yourself. This standoff has to be civil. I see you got some color in you boy, so listen up, cause that's Dr. King talking now!"

The embarrassed guard instructed the transients to move on, then turned to Hattie. "Standoff?" He pulled up a chair, unhooked the radio off his belt and sat down beside the spunky senior.

"Look at you. You must be a hundred years old . . . like my great grandmother."

"You don't say!" Hattie had never visualized herself as a great-grandmother type. "Tell me son, does she have any hopes or dreams left in her?"

He nodded. "Yeah, she designs women's scarves. Talks about opening a scarf shop in Brooklyn."

Hattie bit into the string cheese. "Why doesn't she?"

Potente shrugged. The question made him think. "Don't really know. Too old, I guess. Takes money to do it "

He noticed Hattie's disapproval and explained.

"That's most of the problem. She's feisty, always looking for the angle. It's kind of a family joke, Grandma B scheming her way into the New York garment trade!"

"You mean *she's* a family joke!"

The young man looked down. "Now she's forgetting a bunch of things, Miss Plain. That doesn't help."

"Well I'd forget too if I was shut up in a box because I was considered useless." Hattie gazed at the employees heading across the lobby. "Too old, humph! No such thing. You know they start telling you those lies when you're in your forties!"

Potente's radio crackled. He turned away and spoke cryptically.

"In contact with subject, stand by." He turned to her.

"You know, I'm just going to tell them I can't handle you with safety." He stood up. "Looks like I'm the one that can't win here."

Hattie stuffed the cheese wrapper in her purse.

"What is that gonna mean to your job, son?"

"I'll get written up, reassigned, maybe." He shrugged. "Or quit."

Oh no!" Hattie shook her finger at him. "You won't lose your situation over me, no sir, I will not let you do that. You'll tell them the truth, Ricky Potente, and be proud of the job you're doing. I'm not going anywhere, and there's not a damn thing your bosses or their bosses can do about it. Choose your battles wisely young man and you'll have history and the Almighty on your side."

The guard rolled his eyes. "I don't know what to do with you. Hug you or shoot you."

"Mr. Potente," Hattie grinned. "It's all about doing the right thing the right way at the right time."

The security guard re-attached the walkie-talkie to his belt.

"I'll be back Miss Plain. What can I tell them you want?"

"I want to see Mr. James Pierce." Hattie shook her cane vigorously. "You can tell them I ain't going anywhere till that happens."

"Mr. Pierce?" Potente grimaced. "You sure? He's like the big kahuna in this organization."

"You want decisions, you go to people who can make them, Officer Potente." She banged her cane on the floor. "Remember that."

Ricky Potente stood at the elevator, listening for the approach of the ascending car. As the doors opened, he cast one more look at the cane-wielding old woman who was causing him to think again about so many things.

Chapter 8

August 9, 1951
Editor, Sadie Says
New York Daily Record

Dear Sadie,

My husband passed on recently. His insurance company was notified, but months went by and I heard nothing from them. I wrote the second time, included a copy of his death certificate, and still no response. The agent that sold us the policy had moved away years ago. I took the paperwork and went to the Insurance Company Headquarters, a ninety-minute bus trip from our town. I explained to the receptionist why I had come. I sat there humiliated for six more hours and finally a clerk came out and said I'd have to come back another day, they couldn't find my husband's file. Two more weeks went by. Yesterday I received a form letter from them saying the company had merged with another company and all policies would be re-issued under the new name. Not a word about my claim! I'm about to see a lawyer, but what do you think I should do? Signed, Disappointed

Dear Disappointed,

    Rule number one, never present your case to the wrong person. Relate your story to a real vice-president of customer relations and tell him you'll be addressing the issue next with the New York Insurance Commissioner, and then the New York Daily Record whose Features Editor will be tickled to expose their slothful ways in the popular Sunday edition.
Sadie

Dear Sadie,

    I did as you said. A week after I spoke to the Vice President, a cashier's check for the entire amount was rushed by courier to my house. Thank God for you.
    Happy-under-the-circumstances

Hattie was lost in thought, the story of Potente's great-grandmother much on her mind.

"Mrs. Plain?"

Hattie jumped. She turned and saw a thin young man wearing long curls, a bow tie and a white shirt. She somehow knew he wasn't James Pierce. "What you want with me?"

"I'm Darryl Sykes. From HR."

Hattie had to smile. Young Sykes was not afraid to wear a bow tie. "Alright."

"I've been watching and listening." He seemed apprehensive. "Just so you'll know, there's been a big cutback here. Lots of people are cleaning out their desks. This isn't exactly the perfect time to be getting on board. Nothing personal."

"Humph. I asked that Mallory woman for the Department Editor, I get Darryl from Human Resources. Now answer me this, Mr. Sykes, those people losing their jobs, what one thing do they have in common?"

Darryl Sykes produced a folded piece of paper from his suit pocket. "Ah, I'm not sure."

Hattie pulled on a lock of her own gray hair. "They're all fifty or better. Check it out."

"Jobs are disappearing here, Mrs. Plain." He offered the paperwork to Hattie.

"Here, I've brought you an application to take with you." He looked around. "I'm doing this on my own."

Hattie's attitude fell. "Paperwork? That's all you got, Mr. Sykes?" She shook her finger at the young man. "You and I both know there's real hiring going on right here, right now. Son, this newspaper may be changin' but it ain't going out of business. And people still gonna run it." She softened her tone. "Thing is, young people can't run a proper Advice Column. Nothing personal."

Sykes folded the application back into the pocket. "I can't get into specific hiring and retention standards with you, Mrs. Plain."

"Standards, huh." Hattie chuckled. "I talked with your boss. Man wouldn't tell me his name! Who was looking the other way when he got hired?"

Darryl broke into a sheepish grin. "I think they only know how to size up newspaper people. They sort of guess at the rest of us." He looked around. "Okay, Miss Whitefield said you brought a resume?

Hattie patted the sack. "Right here."

"Looks kind of heavy. May I see it?"

"No, you cannot." Hattie sat back. "You don't look like James Pierce to me."

Sykes lowered the file. "Did you say no?"

"You want to know the first rule son? Don't ever give your information to the wrong person. You might wind up dead of old age in somebody's lobby."

The young man thought for a moment. "Wrong person? Interesting. Never thought of it that way. On the other hand, don't be too hasty to turn down the newspaper's only remaining employment rep, Mrs. Plain."

"You can drop the Mrs. Do I look like a blushing bride to you?" Hattie reached into the bag and withdrew a stack of spiral-bound notebooks, plus a sheaf of typed pages. "Well, this is it. My Witness Tree."

"This is a resume? More like a diary or a story." He thumbed through the typewritten pages. "Essays on Life?"

Hattie sat back. "I wrote these over the years, you know, and submitted them to newspapers." She chortled. "Mainly this newspaper."

"Any luck?"

"None here." Hattie lowered her voice. "A few in the Hattiesburg, Mississippi Caller. First one was July 3, 1926." She paused. "I was thirteen. A few got published now and again. Last one in 1929, when I was 16. That was it."

"What is a Witness Tree, Miss Plain?"

Hattie crossed her two index fingers. "Back home you grow a Hickory tree where the property lines come together, honey. Called a Witness tree. So as there would never be confusion about the boundary."

She ran her hand over one of the five notebooks. "See, these mark out where I begin and everybody else leaves off."

Darryl shrugged. "Well, they're going to expect a regular resume."

Hattie appealed. "These pages are full of the information this newspaper will need to properly evaluate me for that job Darryl Sykes. Ain't that what a résumé's supposed to do?"

"Well..." Sykes stood. "There's really nothing I can do."

Hattie secured the heavy bag. "I rest my case."

The ringing phones and computer keyboards had gone quiet. Sykes checked his watch.

"It's five-twenty Miss Plain, and this lobby is going to be packed in ten minutes." He straightened his tie. "You coming back tomorrow?"

"No, Darryl Sykes." Hattie sang softly, "I'm planted by the rivers of water."

"I'm sorry?"

Hattie folded her shawl and nestled it behind her. "An old Gospel song, Mr. Sykes. It means I ain't leaving here tonight without the interview!"

"Well, HR is working late tonight." He raised an eyebrow and pointed at Humphries office. "Processing seven more terminations. Including our staff photographer, Matt Perez. And he's the best we have." The young man sighed. "You see, it isn't as simple as you may think Miss Plain." He stood. "Nice talking with you."

Hattie nodded and watched employees file through the lobby on their way home. Half an hour later the floor was nearly empty.

Hattie brought out another unopened card from her bag. It was from Lovae, Bobbi's daughter. She would be over seventy now. The card was simple, a free-form depiction of mother and infant. Inside a practiced hand had written,

"Happy 92d Birthday, Hattie, it may take a hundred more years so don't make any plans. God bless you and the child,

Lovae."

My Saddest Day
An Essay by Miriam Jones
April 14 1929

My father Rupert Jones went to jail on an assault charge yesterday. The special one-

page handout which Mr. Davis and I wrote, and which was distributed to nearly everybody in East Hattiesburg, was unfortunately about to hurt us all. I was working that Sunday at the press, my last day to set up type and ink the rollers, as I was about to begin my new job as a newspaper reporter. Well a mob of angry men came near to dinnertime and called out Mr. Davis. They had axes and torches, lanterns, rope and the like. I am just sixteen years old and scared to death. What had we done to rile them so?

Mr. Davis handed me the can of donations, almost twenty-five dollars, which had come in. Then he hugged me and thanked me for all my work and told me to never abandon my dreams. He ordered me to run home to Palmers Crossing fast as I could using the back streets and the forest, so as nobody could see me. He waved me off, then turned and grabbed something off the wall. Then that sainted man stepped out the front door.

I hid behind a rain barrel. Mr. Davis stood and held up his framed copy of the First Amendment and asked if anybody knew what it meant. No one knew I guess, because they hanged Mr. Ponce Davis from the second story window of his building.

Chapter 9

Hattie drew out the sepia toned family portrait and set it on her legs. The overhead lighting favored the delicate beauty of her mother Oswega Pullman Jones, and the proud almond eyes of her daddy Rupert Grant Jones, his jaw set and head raised, his nappy hair slightly billowed on top and sides. On the back a faded pencil legend noted, "Born Oswega Pullman Jeffries July 4, 1879, Palmers Crossing Mississippi, daughter of Edwina and Horace."

The couple lived at the end of a dirt road in a shotgun style house. Oswega's brother Alphonse relocated to New York City in 1905 and became a messenger for Western Union. He corresponded with his sister by sending her occasional copies of the New York Times, which Oswega efficiently used as wall paper in the bungalow. It would become a daily education for their only daughter.

Both Oswega and Rupert talked endlessly about going North to New York where the economy permitted a good wage, according to the newspaper's Help Wanted ads. There Miriam could receive a good education. But the hand-to-mouth existence of the lumber slab puller didn't include the luxury of saving travel money.

Hattie studied the girl's face. Miriam was especially bright and attractive. In the ancient photograph, her face shown with great energy. Her complexion was even, her slightly oval eyes sparkled with hope, and the easy smile was contagious.

Hattie recalled men always paid attention to Miriam from the earliest age, and she would always blush when they mentioned her beauty. By thirteen she developed a womanly figure, a further source of public embarrassment.

If only a girl's mind and body, emotions and ambitions would blossom on the same day, she wrote in an unpublished letter on her fifteenth birthday, *there would be fewer people and more progress.*

An hour passed. The elevator opened, and out stepped Guards Breen and Potente pushing a wheelchair, accompanied by a striking redhead in her mid-thirties, dressed in Armani and black pearls. Her stiletto heels pounded the tiles like tack hammers.

She marched into the foyer and saw the old woman seated by the drinking fountain holding the Wal-Mart sack. She looked back at Potente. It seemed incredulous to her this centurion could be any real trouble. But intelligence didn't lie.

She announced crisply, "Mr. Humphries, please stand by."

The bespeckled Humphries emerged again from his cubicle.

"Are we ready to toss her?"

Potente shot a glance at him. "Hey Mr. Humphries, show some respect."

Humphries slipped his suit coat on. "Feeling free to call me out now, Potente?"

"Pay attention please," Albrecht snapped. "I'm already late to something very important."

Hattie stood leaning on her cane.

The well-dressed woman pointed at Breen. "Okay. Give her the particulars, Sergeant."

Guard Breen addressed Hattie. "Miss Hattie Plain, you are trespassing. You have repeatedly refused to follow our rules and warnings. You will remain in our custody until a New York City Police Officer comes for you. Please sit down in this wheelchair and offer no further resistance."

Hattie looked over the woman. "Security I understand. HR I understand. But who in the world are you?"

The glamorous woman fastened her eyes on Hattie Plain.

"Lonnie Albrecht, Executive Vice-President, Corporate Operations. I'm witnessing this event. In case of a lawsuit."

Hattie leveled a firm gaze. "I ain't here to sue you, Miss Albrecht."

The owner looked Hattie up and down. "Funny, we just received a call from an editor at the Times asking about you. A man named Benson something or other? Apparently, you worked over there as a janitor for decades, and now you're here looking to run our features page?"

Lonnie glanced at the guards. "Okay gentlemen, try to be gentle."

The two guards each took an arm, but Hattie instantly jerked away. Her cane slipped and she lost her balance. Potente reached out to hold her up but his strong grip caused her to howl. Then Hattie went to the floor. Breen kicked the chair away and bent over the prostrate woman, attempting to attach plastic cuffs to her flailing arms.

Lonnie bent over to recover Hattie's cane. That's when she noticed Perez taking pictures with his phone.

"Wow!" Matt was smiling. "Took all four of you, but you finally brought her down."

The two hapless guards helped Hattie to her feet. Her bound wrists were turning purple from bruising. Glasses hung from her disheveled face.

A group of curious employees watched as Perez flipped open his cell phone and pressed buttons. Lonnie Albrecht cursed under her breath.

"Alright people, leave the lobby, and go home please." She addressed the photographer. "Matt. Give me the camera."

Perez closed his phone. "What, Miss Albrecht? You want to take my private images in my private phone?"

Lonnie folded her arms. "You'll not last long here with that attitude Matt." She barked at Breen. "Security, relieve Mr. Perez of his camera."

The husky sergeant stepped forward and Perez reluctantly handed him the instrument. Breen presented it to Lonnie.

Hattie held out her arms to have the cuffs removed.

"He's just witnessing, like you. And me. Except he ain't in cuffs."

Perez shook his head. "I got my pink slip two weeks ago, Lonnie. This is my last day, not that you care. You want the truth? If your family didn't own this place, you'd be in the unemployment line." Perez gestured at the lobby. "You're running this paper right into the ground."

Lonnie erased the digital images on the camera while eyeing the photographer with obvious loathing. "I'm surprised Matt. All this time I thought you were different. But you're just another mindless whore with a lens. You actually bite the hand that feeds you. You make me sick."

Matt Perez laughed. "Sick? For seven years, six of them good, this paper survived on my pictures. I won four photographic awards and got your paper two more. You and your family got rich off my work. Mathew Brady I ain't, Lonnie... but a whore? You should talk! I'll take my camera please."

Lonnie Albrecht slapped the camera into his outstretched hand. "Goodbye, Matt." She turned to Hattie who was tugging on her disheveled dress.

"You have brought this on yourself. Miss Plain. You know, there is a great threat today posed by passed-over people who create chaos while executing their private agendas. Gathering intelligence, for example. How perfect, an old lady looking to 'interview' with the paper that wouldn't publish her... whatever it is you write."

Potente stepped up. "Miss Albrecht, I don't believe this old lady is a spy, she's just trying to live out a dream."

"Remember what you just said, Potente." Humphries lectured. "It's the reason you'll always be a security guard."

Lonnie turned to Breen. "Officer Breen, take her in to General Offices and run a background. Use the EPB database. She's obviously being used by the Times to report on our changes. I really didn't know they were that worried. That Times editor who called here, what was his last name?"

Hattie shook her head. "You are out of your mind."

Potente thought for a moment. "Ridges, Benson Ridges."

"Good. Get *his* story too." She turned to Potente. "Okay. everything changes now. Call off the NY cops, we have our own investigating to do. And I have a critical dinner to cancel."

She grabbed Humphries by the arm. "Mr. Humphries, get hold of Earl Hudson in IT and the two of you escort our visitor to security, while Guard Potente sees Matt to the door. He'll join you when he gets a fix on this Benson Ridges character."

She nodded at Potente as she stormed out of the hallway. "Let me know when you've got the data."

Potente took Breen aside. "Ms. Albrecht said to use the Extended Private Background inquiry service. What's this poor old woman done to deserve this kind of scrutiny?" Breen was dismissive.

"Just get on line. Follow orders."

Potente escorted the photographer Mat Perez into the elevator and the doors shut.

Breen looked at Hattie who was still catching her breath.

"This way, lady."

In the windowless security suite, the near-centurion was guided to a couch next to a dusty Fichus tree. The opposite door opened into the IT equipment center where Breen and Humphries watched with interest as Hudson brought up the Internet files on a suspicious mop-slinger from the New York Times.

Chapter 10

Local Notes

by Benson Ridges, NY Times Special Features Editor

July 1964 Lennox Park

Voter Registration Group Plans Rally

The Reverend Sinclair Padgett of <u>*Register First!*</u> *, a national civil rights group, brought his Freedom Riders recruitment rally to New York this week. The minister plans to enlist volunteers from New York to bus themselves into the target state of Mississippi for the purpose of registering potential voters. The Harlem rally will be held Saturday July 4. Police said parade permits had been sought for a march to City Hall.*

Spokesman Abraham Ford said the group is modeled after the non-violent organizing strategy of Dr. Martin Luther King. Padgett, a long-time radio gospel preacher, is expected to preach and to find local speakers as well.

Hattie closed her eyes and recaptured the memories. A month before the rally a flyer had been placed at

Hattie's door seeking testimonies of former residents of Mississippi. For the first time in 35 years, her Hattiesburg history seemed needed.

Although uneasy about reopening the memories, Hattie was drawn to the larger idea and volunteered to come forward and discuss her experiences publicly.

Her assigned escort for the civil rights event was the New York group coordinator Abraham Ford, a graduate student of CCNY. On a Friday morning in June, he and Hattie walked the two blocks to East Harlem Park, accompanied by Ruthie and Lovae in her wheel chair.

**

The throng was greater than anticipated and caution was in the air. Rioting had broken out in several northern cities that summer. The very presence of helmeted policemen signaled the nervousness of the NY City political establishment.

"The times are tense enough," Abraham told Hattie. "We don't need more gasoline on the fire, we need soldiers of peace in the field."

Lovae pushed along in her chair. "Once poor people are registered, how will they know who to vote for?"

"Our future leaders haven't even been born yet, Lovae. The battle may be a hundred years long, this is just the opening salvo."

The podium stood atop a hastily constructed platform, draped with green cloth. Large speakers pointed at the gradual green slope where several hundred people had already gathered in the late morning heat. But Mayor Wagner and the borough alderman were not yet present.

The crowd was stirring as the temperature rose, and an hour past kickoff still no one from Tammany Hall had arrived. At Ford's signal the taped musical program stopped and the plump Padgett took the microphone. The gathering hushed.

"Brothers and Sisters!" he began. "There is a new day at hand, let me tell you about it. This morning the sun rose on an America where there's some of us living free and some of us still in bondage to the Pharaoh of Bigotry. Still subject to that old devil of oppression."

Murmurs rippled across the growing assembly. Padgett's voice rose. "God himself has declared that old dragon illegal, don't you know."

The crowd response swelled.

Immoral!" The preacher's voice shook as he brought his arm down. "And ready to fall!"

The roar filled the park. Hattie found herself clapping.

"Now the weapons of our warfare are not guns, not batons nor vicious dogs! Not fire hoses!"

Chants of *amen* came from hundreds of voices.

"No, the weapons of our warfare are not carnal, but *Mighty* through God…"

The cheer began to rise again. Hattie found herself thinking of Mr. Davis and his beloved newspaper.

"To the pulling down of strongholds!"

Chants of *Freedom Now, Freedom Now* arose in the field. The Reverend boomed, "Casting down oppression and slavery, second-class citizenship, bringing them that sit in darkness out of the prison house, oh a great light has shined!"

Clapping spread throughout the crowd with shouts of amen. Hattie was on her feet.

"And we know that every knee shall bow to justice! There will be no exceptions!"

Chanting began again. A swaying Hattie sang in unison and clapped in rhythm.

"And every free man and free woman in this country will go to the polls and cast a vote for whosoever he or she chooses! With no exceptions! That is the moral and constitutional law!"

The preacher stood back as the inspired assembly broke into the mantra *Freedom Now*. Padgett again seized the mike with both hands. "But wait!" he roared.

The crowd went quiet.

"Our brothers and our sisters can't get to the poles, no they can't stand up and be counted. The devil has put barriers in the way, illegal tests, chains on their feet! They suffer for speaking out!"

Groaning began.

"But let me ask you something . . . are they alone?"

The throng responded in the negative.

"That's right," he continued, blotting sweat from his forehead. "They are not alone. Huh. Our people need to know," he waved his arm at the crowd, "there is an entire country of angels behind their aspirations, huh, a mighty force of decent soldiers, huh, willing to get on the bus, huh, and travel to their cities, huh, and villages, huh, preaching the gospel of free elections and self-government! Oh angels, come register them to vote!"

Applause grew.

Hattie closed her eyes. She could easily see a hundred busses pulling into Hattiesburg. Hordes of Registrars and US Marshals would swamp the band of bullies led by Ketchum and Thatcher. Her people would rally, their political voice would prevail and change would surely come to Hattiesburg. Children would finally have a chance. She hummed "God Bless the Child." Bring them on.

Padgett paced the podium. "Our people need that light, they're waiting on it, and they're ready to live for it and ready to die for it!"

The crowd roared.

"Cause they know one thing for sure, they gonna die without it!"

Approval noise across the field heightened.

Hattie noticed on the far edge of the park mounted police and weaponized vehicles were assembling.

"Are you ready to help?" Padgett threw open his arms as shouts of support reflected back.

"Are you willing to get on a bus?"

Voices subsided.

Hattie felt her fingers go cold. Time had almost come. Her heart began thumping. Panic was rising. She had never addressed a real assembly of people with an important message. The newspaper did that for her.

Padgett was closing his remarks. "But for now, to those who create and maintain the millstone of discrimination in this beloved city on the hill, I say one thing!" Chanting began gain. "I say how beautiful upon the mountains are the feet of him that bringeth good tidings, that *publisheth peace!*"

He turned to her. "Hattie Plain, escapee of hate, survivor of massacre, messenger of hope, come, talk to us!"

As she stood, the preoccupied visiting speaker could barely hear the crowd's thunderous reaction. She felt the spirit of Ponce Davis sweep through her. Once again, his sacrifice was fresh. His legacy was alive in her. She would be his voice today.

In the press pit Benson Ridges climbed a table to see Hattie better. He cut a lean figure in his generously cut Hong Kong suit. His light brown hair was a mass of tight waves. Thick bifocals and a long nose accentuated his triangular shaped face. He held a clipboard and pencil, and smiled as he and Hattie briefly touched glances.

He watched the proud woman work her way to the mic where Padgett stood beaming. Applause was building. Ridges leaned into a speaker to hear any exchange between Hattie and Padgett. He scribbled notes as Padgett pressed her hands and whispered loudly.

"Bring me a full bus, sister!"

"I'm not good at this Reverend," she whispered back "I ain't nothing but a janitor."

Ridges recorded Padgett's reply as he pressed the mike into her trembling hand. "I believe you got just the background we need, Miss Plain."

Chapter 11

**

In the IT room, three men stared at the wide computer monitor. Hudson scratched his head.

"I still don't get it. We only use the Extended Personal Background program for high profilers or suspect employees." He ran a pencil through a heavy brown moustache. "Why *are* we using it on her?"

Breen shot back. "Cause Ms. Albrecht wants it done, geek, and she signs your checks. Get on it."

Potente returned from escorting the photographer Perez, and glanced at Hattie sitting on the couch in the other room.

"Hudson's got a point Breen. Lonnie's acting weirder every day if you ask me. People know it too, brother."

"Analyzing executives?" Humphries looked over Potente. "Is that what Security Guards get paid for now?"

"It's not that hard, Mr. Humphries. Look around."

"Are you suggesting the family that founded this paper and ran it like a watch for nearly seventy years have become a bunch of incompetents?"

Ricky Potente watched the screen morph. "Since the family turned the paper over to her last year, things have gone downhill, Mr. Humphries. That's what I hear anyway. The pressure's really on this poor guy Pierce to turn it around."

Breen grunted. "This 'poor' guy makes more in one year than I make in ten. You want pressure, try raising three kids in Jersey on a guard's salary."

Hudson leaned forward. "OK we're in. What's the subject's name again? Hat-tie Pl-ain…We have a Social Security number or anything? No? This will take a while to access. Looks like a big file."

"It'll take a minute to print."

"Okay," said Potente with a tinge of regret. "I'll tell Miss Albrecht we're almost ready."

**

Dec 3, 1981
Editor, Jamie's Jumpin'
New York Daily Record

Dear Jamie,

Last year you told Miserable in Missouri to stop each day and be grateful for something. That seemed impossible to me. You see, my children were taken from me by the state because of false accusations by a neighbor who hated me. I paid lawyers until I had no more money. I was fired because of the resultant absenteeism. I had no relatives and friends were hard to find. Well I just wanted to write you and say I started the program of gratitude. Every day I would find something to be grateful for! It was difficult at first. But it became a habit, and my attitude changed, and therefore attitudes toward me changed. New friends appeared. I was re-hired for more money, I found a wonderful man and my children were eventually returned. Gratitude has restored the years that the locust (self-pity) has eaten!

  Healed in Hoboken

**

Holding his notes, Potente knocked on Lonnie's office door, and stepped into the plush executive suite. "Miss Albrecht, I have that info on the *Times* caller."

"Good." She looked up from her massive desk, her thin Brows arched. "Planning to share it?"

Potente looked through his notes quickly. "Name is Benson Ridges, night shift Assistant Managing Editor. Old guy. Pretty much built in over there. Reportedly connected to the paper's founders."

"Really!" Lonnie smirked, pressing together her bejeweled fingers. "I'm surprised people so high up would stoop so low for so little."

Potente scanned the document. "Definite past connections with the subject. Nothing too obvious. He appeared to pull some strings for her at various times. Friends maybe. Or more. Still looking into it."

"Pulled strings, eh." Lonnie got up from her desk. "Do you suppose our string-pulling friend, part of the founding family, is probing our paper through this so-called charwoman for some reason?"

"Could be, Miss Albrecht." Potente handed her the file. "But why?"

"Oh, I don't know. Suppose someone wanted to invest in this paper, Officer Potente, and the Times got a whiff. Wouldn't they want to know current media values? Maybe discredit us so the buyer would have second thoughts?"

Potente followed closely as they crossed the marble foyer. "Miss Albrecht, are you selling this newspaper?"

"Did I say I was selling? I'm thinking, officer Potente. Healthy speculation, now forget it." Lonnie headed for the door. "Okay. Time to turn up the heat."

Entering the Security suite, Potente stayed just behind Lonnie. She walked right up to the octogenarian still sitting on the divan next to the Fichus and empty desk.

"Miss Plain, what is your connection with Benson Ridges at the *Times?*"

Hattie sat a little straighter. Her colorful dress and sequined hat gave her the endearing look of a warm grand-mother, but her dark, candid eyes held Lonnie's stare with determination.

"I asked him to check up on my progress in gettin this interview. My reference."

"You mean you worked for him?" Lonnie's sharpened tone gave rise to her suspicions. "You have the same *interests?*"

Potente softened the tone. "Or do you simply mean he can vouch for you?"

Hattie closed her eyes for a moment. "I mean to say that man can teach the world something about equal opportunities ..."

Lonnie scoffed. "Oh, please don't spin this as a civil rights issue, Miss Plain. You're an interloper, pure and simple." She stepped back with folded arms and stared at the old woman in disgust. "God, this is distasteful."

Humphries entered. "Extended search ready?"

Lonnie noted Hattie's reaction to Humphry's question. The old spy was nervous and would crack before this was over. Humphries continued. "The name Hattie Plain first appears in September 1929, where she was a suspect in the death of two men in Tennessee, same month arrested for being a public nuisance in New York."

Breen sat forward. His fat neck rolled over his shirt collar.

"Mr. Humphries, did you just say she killed two men in Tennessee?"

Lonnie sighed. "No Breen, he said she was a suspect."

Potente looked at the group. "Black people were always suspects. Cold-blooded murder? Please. What was she, sixteen? C'mon man."

"Oh, it's about being black?" Breen was dismissive. "Typical liberal, defending her without knowing a damn thing."

"Is that right?" Potente leveled a cold look at Breen.

"I talked with her, hero. I already know more than all of you put together."

"Can it." Albrecht nodded at Humphries. "Continue."

The bald man adjusted his glasses. "Okay, hospital report shows her having a baby in NYC 1929, then reporting it as dead in 1931. Whoa! Committed to New York Mental Institute 1935. Out in a few weeks. Then another baby in 1939. Husband killed in the war 1944. Police arrests begin in 1953 and go on long as my arm."

Breen was curious. "Arrests? Like what?"

Potente scowled. "What is that to you, Breen?"

"Details please." Lonnie looked at Humphries. "What was it, fraud? Blackmail? Bribery? Let's hear it all, we paid for it."

Humphries went on. "Busted four times, prostitution '53 to '58. Arrested for possession of controlled substance, 1963. Arrested six times between 1963 and 1971 for disorderly conduct, failure to obey a lawful order." He glanced up. "Well, Grandma, you're a trip!"

"Let me see that." Lonnie took the sheets from Humphries and quickly scanned. "Here's something . . . her son was killed by police, September 64. Suspect in a robbery attempt at Trudy's Ribs in Harlem. She sued the Police for Wrongful Death, won a hundred K settlement."

Breen whistled. "A hundred large. In the sixties! Man, that was money then."

"It's money now, Breen." Potente rubbed his face. "Not that you'll ever know."

Breen stood and pointed. "Hey, I'm not locked in to this crap job forever, buddy. I got plans."

Lonnie glanced at him. "Good."

Humphries fastened his eyes on the old woman. "I wonder what she did with the money?"

Chapter 12

**

Summer 1964, East Harlem Park

Hattie Plain reluctantly took the microphone. Looking out on the sea of faces, she shuddered with trepidation. Benson Ridges waved from his table. Lovae and Ruthie were near. Abraham stood by, beaming.

Hattie imagined Mr. Davis in the front row and a faint smile crossed her face. In that moment her voice soared.

"My people!"

A loud cheer went up immediately. Hattie waved. "I'm happy today that there was not a Freedom Rider come to my town of Hattiesburg almost forty years ago, yes you heard me, I am *glad*."

Silence descended on the park.

"You see he'd surely be dead in that town." She paused. "Instead, I wish there had been a hundred Freedom Riders! Or a thousand!"

Voices roared. Abraham, surveying the crowd from his seat on the podium, observed police cars converging at the park entrance.

Hattie's voice cracked as her thoughts flooded with memories of her mentor.

"The most decent man I have ever met, Mr. Ponce Davis, gave his life to spreading literacy and hope to black share-croppers and mill workers around Hattiesburg, Mississippi. He printed a newspaper by hand, and then taught his people how to read it.

"Under the noses of the Klan itself he spoke softly for seventy years. Then one day they came for him, lynched him, and incinerated his newspaper."

The crowd feedback rumbled low and negative.

Hattie continued. "I saw it happen, so they went after me, slaughtered my parents and burned our house to the ground. Praise God, I escaped."

The booing swept through the mass of attendees. "But now it's time to return to Hattiesburg! Not me! You!"

She paused as the idea sunk in.

With perfect timing, she continued. "Not with nooses but with registrations and elections. Not with revenge but with hope! The time has come for you to get up here and stand with Reverend Padgett and say 'Yes! I want to march into the belly of that beast, I want to register voters! There's children in Mississippi yearning to be free, I'll free them! There's men and women languishing in self-loathing, I'll free them! I'll put on the armor of God and enter the viper's den and I'll not fear for nothin' because I'll be doing the *right* thing!"

The crowd roared back. *"Do it now! Do it now!"*

Hattie handed Reverend Padgett the microphone.

"Thank you, Hattie." He leaned in. "You quite a speaker!" Padgett welcomed two young men filing onto the rostrum. Abraham spoke briefly to each, then ushered the first volunteer to Padgett's side.

The preacher boomed, "You scc already the Lord has touched the hearts of these two brave men, And I see more on the way, c'mon up here! Brother Abraham will get your contact information." The first man leaned nervously into the mike. "I'm Jewish," he yelled into the mic. "But today I'm also you! And I'm on my way to Mississippi!"

Voices on the green erupted in support.

The second young man took the microphone and waited for the cheering to wane. "Me, I'm red, white and blue. I am America and Miss Plain, you can tell them I'll be on that bus!"

Padgett's voice rose against the swelling shouting. "We just heard two young men claim their readiness to board a Freedom bus! We are moved by our sister Hattie as she tells us of the Klan's criminal and inhumane behavior she was forced to witness. I look out and see a thousand citizens here today in support of freedom. But then I look around and notice all the empty chairs supposed to be filled with our own city leadership, empty! *Empty!*"

Police lines now surrounded the exits.

Padgett smiled broadly. "Brothers and sisters let's take a walk right on down to City Hall and see just why our elected servants couldn't be here today!"

The field of listeners applauded with delight.

Abraham signaled the guards and ushers to maintain peace as the ebullient crowds moved toward the street. Then he noticed the line of helmets and batons. He waved at Padgett but the preacher wasn't looking his way.

The big man bolted for the mic and blurted out, "Slow it down, brothers!" From the stage he could see mounted police forming a new line. Abraham yelled at the top of his lungs, "You got to stop for a minute!"

Jumping from the platform, he sprinted toward the danger zone. Behind him boomed the unmistakable voice of Reverend Padgett.

"Peacefully brothers! Let the angels lead you today!"

The big man squeezed through the surging crowd and found a police lieutenant standing behind the line. The officer's visor was down and he held a white-knuckle grip on his baton while staying glued to the collar-mounted radio. His second-in-command stood with him.

Ford waved a pink document. The noise level was rising and he shouted to be understood.

"Officer, we have a parade permit!"

No one heard him.

"We have a permit!" he yelled again, holding up the blue paperwork.

The commander raised his protective visor. "You got no permit to disturb the peace, boy. Get'm under control or we'll do it for you."

Officers pushed by Ford, shouting orders to form a wedge. Handheld loudspeakers blared. Then out of nowhere a rock glanced off the commander's helmet. The adjutant barked into his radio and the human wedge began moving, weapons brandished.

Abraham spun around and took the Lieutenant by his shoulder. "Brother, please…"

Suddenly Ford was tackled from behind. A squad of uniforms flipped him on his stomach and pinned him there in the grass with a boot in his back and one on his neck. Pain made him squirm, bringing baton blows upon his head and neck.

He heard Ruth's frantic voice above the noise, "I'm comin', baby, hold on."

Abraham struggled to yell, but his appeals for order were muffled as dirt filled his open mouth.

From the podium Hattie saw Abraham's take-down, and grabbed the open mic.

"Stop, stop!" she hollered. The forty-ish speaker hurried off the platform and began racing toward the Lennox Street staging area with Lovae next to her in the chair. Both women screamed to be heard above the deafening pitch.

"Stop! Sit down! Peace!"

Hattie realized the peace rally was now a full-blown riot and fought her way forward to reach her fallen escort. Lovae dodged the chaos to keep up with her.

"Don't fight!" the crippled woman screamed as she made her way more deeply into the milieu. "Lay down, go to jail!" Standing on a barrier Ruth saw Abraham go down and yelled.

"Hattie, he's down. They knocked Abraham down!" Ruth launched herself into the fray. "I'm comin' baby, hold on!"

A gas grenade landed a few yards away, followed by a loud eruption from the crowd. Order collapsed. Ruth went down, crushed by the sudden retreat of the crowd.

Police advanced, swinging nightsticks. As Lovae rose from her chair to spot Ruth, a baton cracked across her shoulders. Hattie caught her, and turned to the mounted officer with tears of anger flowing down her face. "Damn you! Damn you!"

Hattie helped Lovae back into her chair, and stumbled forward toward the fallen giant, as he struggled to his feet. Tracks of tears ran down his dusty face. "Jesus help us today."

Ruth was now sitting numbly on the field as fleeing demonstrators buffeted her. Her mouth hung open and her eyes remained half-shut.

An explosive thud sounded nearby, and momentarily a second canister landed behind them. A hissing sound was followed by a plume of noxious smoke. It was a hammer blow to Hattie's lungs. Her eyes stung fiercely. Grabbing Ruth, she collapsed on Ford, seeking air near the ground.

Lovae, unable to breathe, fell on the three of them and there they remained huddled until police came through and separated them.

Within an hour Hattie Plain held Lovae in the back of a Paddy Wagon as two hundred marchers headed for central booking in an armada of busses.

The booking sergeant informed Hattie that someone from the *New York Times* made bail for Hattie, Ruth and Lovae.

A limousine drew up and the unfamiliar driver offered to return the trio back to 125th Street but after a short discussion, the offer was declined.

Lovae, although injured, was able to sit in her chair, Ruthie was still traumatized but recovering, and Hattie needed to walk off the gas attack.

The would-be benefactor sat in the limo's back seat, looking at Hattie through the smoke colored window. There would have to be another way. And another day.

** **

Potente took Lonnie aside. "Look, Miss Albrecht, you should know that I called him."

Lonnie's forehead wrinkled. "You called who?"

"I called Ridges at the Times." Potente shrugged. "You wanted info and there was no other quicker way to get it. Tell you the truth, he was quite nice to me. A little fancy maybe, but okay to talk to."

Breen snickered. "What did the old fruitcake have to say to you, *Ricky?*"

Lonnie glared at Breen. "These are times that separate men from jerks, Breen. Make your choice before you leave tonight." She played with her notes. "I don't suppose your friend admitted sending a spy in here while they reorganize their own moth-eaten department."

Potente raised his eyebrows. "He just said Hattie would be the best advice editor we could ever find if we were smart enough to hire her."

Lonnie sat back. "Great. What else?"

Potente suddenly remembered. "Oh, he thanked us for the referral of Jumpin' Jamie, says she'll no doubt work out well."

Lonnie wheeled around. "We recommended Jamie to the Times?" She held her head. "Okay, what else?"

"He *suggested* it would be best if Hattie received every courtesy in this process."

"Process? A warning from the Times? Okay, is that it?"

"One more thing." Potente lowered his voice. "Miss Albrecht, apparently Ridges has pictures of Hattie Plain being assaulted by our security people, and wants our side of the story before he publishes them."

"What!" Lonnie threw up her arms. "He's trying to blackmail us with pictures?" The executive kicked a desk. "No way, I took Matt's camera and erased the images myself."

Potente shrugged. "Well apparently not before he emailed them out."

Mallory stuck her head in the door. "Lonnie, there's reporters from the Times and three other papers in the lobby. They all want to talk to Hattie Plain."

Darryl Sykes followed her breathlessly. "Miss Albrecht, USA Today is on line two!"

"I'm not taking calls!" Lonnie Albrecht fired a pen at the wall. "Just what I need, bad press at a bad time!" She spun around and shook her finger at the surprised staff.

"Do not let this get out of control! Do you all hear me?" Elizabeth Whitefield ran in. "Quick! Turn on CNN!"

Chapter 13

**

September 1964

"Hattie, turn on your television!" Ruth was yelling from her window. "Hattie!" She thumped on the floor.

The noise awakened Hattie from a from a Sunday afternoon nap.

"Hear me, Hattie Plain, turn on your TV!" came the urgent voice. But Hattie's groggy attention instead went to the buzzing of the front door. Visitors were rare these days. She hobbled to the intercom.

"Yes?"

The baritone voice was unmistakable. "Good afternoon Miss Plain, Abraham Ford."

"Ah, Mr. Ford!" Hattie hurried to meet him at the front door. There the colossus stood quietly, head bowed. She had forgotten how imposing this polite young man was.

"Miss Plain," he looked up and Hattie sensed his sorrow. "I hate to bother you on a Sunday afternoon, but could I talk with you for a minute? Inside…"

Hattie invited the solemn Ford into the apartment. He stood by the window. She offered tea, but it was refused.

"Miss Plain, the two young men we sent to Mississippi, well, as you know they met up with another young worker of ours, a Hattiesburg local. They did voter registration work together and went missing together. Been a few weeks now. As you know."

Hattie nodded.

Ford took a deep breath. "Look here, I don't know if you've seen the television . . ."

Hattie's face drained. "No, Mr. Ford, I haven't."

"Ma'am, those missing young men, well they've been found."

Hattie waited, her hand trembling. "Found . . .?"

"Their bodies were discovered by the FBI in Mississippi, ma'am, in a dirt levee."

Hattie and Ford spent a moment in silence. Ford kneeled and spoke quietly.

"The resistance to freedom is stronger and deeper than we calculated, Miss Plain."

"Dear Jesus." Hattie shook her head. "What have I done?"

Ford touched her arm. "You did the right thing."

Hattie opened her hands in helplessness. "I got myself out of that place but sent them right back in, didn't I?"

The guest gently took her hand. "You did the right thing, Miss Plain."

"But Mr. Ford," Hattie struggled to be clear. "I was the one person who had been through it, don't you see? I knew what those young men faced."

Abraham Ford sat quietly for a moment. Then he gazed at Hattie with red-rimmed eyes. "My grandfather and grand-mother were dragged five miles behind a truck eight years ago Miss Plain. There's sorrow to go around."

Hattie searched his sad face through her own tears. "Bless their hearts, son."

Ford stood. "Respectfully ma'am, when the history of this struggle is written, the martyrdom of these three boys will be seen as the tipping point, I know that in my heart." Ford kissed her hand.

"I'll leave you be, Miss Plain."

Rolling back her head to stem the emotional tide, Hattie grabbed Ford's wrist. "Say it with me brother, "For our light affliction, which is but for a moment . . ."

Ford closed his eyes. "Worketh for us a far more exceeding and eternal weight of glory."

Hattie closed her flooded eyes and hummed God Bless the Child.

Abraham Ford found his way out. The elderly refugee from Hattiesburg sat the rest of the day in her living room staring at the window overlooking the great Hickory tree, oblivious to the ringing phone and Ruthie's muffled shouting.

**

Hudson grabbed the remote and all heads turned to the wall-mounted television. Two anchors appeared, cutting to fly-over video of the *Daily Record* building. A voice-over began.

Repeating our top story, the uncorroborated account of ninety-two-year-old Harlem resident Hattie Plain possibly assaulted and allegedly held against her will within the walls of this building which houses the New York Daily Record, one of the city's oldest family-run metro newspapers. When contacted, James Pierce, newly named managing editor, returning from a business trip, said he had no knowledge of this crisis. But he promised to get to the bottom of it quickly. Updates as they happen. In other news. . .

Mallory stood under a ceiling light, her hands on her hips. In the glass partition she could see her reflection. She straightened her posture and pushed hair off her forehead.

"Lonnie," she yelled. "Phones are ringing off the hook!"

Albrecht was on the house phone. "Let them ring, dammit.

"People are threatening their subscriptions," Mallory fumed, "If there's any truth to the story they're hearing. Which of course, there *isn't.*"

Potente leaned in the doorway. "Miss Albrecht, there's a network helicopter flying over our building. And there's a street crowd watching the window news tape on the first floor." He glanced at Breen. "What's next, SWAT?"

Lonnie Albrecht glowered at Mallory. "Corporate communications, right? Isn't that what you do? It's your degree, right?"

Mallory flinched as her boss slammed a book to the floor. "Well you better start communicating, dammit! Here I am ducking the Mayor's calls, who's next! Solve this, *now!*"

"I'll call a press conference." Mallory turned to her desk mirror and practiced a lead-in. "Don't believe this. We're proud to be the most respected . . ."

A beleaguered Lonnie turned to Hattie. "Okay, grandma, it's truth time." She circled in front of the resolute old woman who continued to hold her gaze fearlessly. "What is this about? Let's go. I've giving up a lot to hear this."

Hattie shrugged. "Why you askin' me? That woman right there knows why I'm here. She's the one I told everything to."

"Me?" Mallory reflected on her original conversation with Hattie Plain. Then it dawned on her slowly. "Hey wait a minute. She came in here ready for a fight." She glared at the old charwoman. "Oh my Lord. Have you set us up?"

Albrecht whined. "Good God, lady!" She leaned into Hattie's face. Sweat glistened under the black pearls. *"What do you want?"*

Hattie stood up with one hand on her shopping bag. "I told you what I want."

Mallory whined, "She wants Jamie's old job."

Lonnie circled the couch. "I couldn't put you in that job if I wanted to. It's been reorganized out of existence. Don't you get it? You come waltzing in here planting land mines against us, and expect us to give you a nonexistent job? Is that the real reason you're even here?"

Mallory's snapped her fingers. "Exactly what I told her, Lonnie. In fact… "

Hattie banged her cane on the floor. "I didn't ask for a job!"

There was sudden silence in the room.

Hattie glowered. "I asked for a chance. That's all. An interview."

Mallory now realized her mistake. Maybe she could still correct it. She glanced at Lonnie who stood speechless, her mouth open. Slowly the boss turned to a cowering Mallory.

"This all goes away with an interview?" she hissed. "And you *knew* it?"

Mallory tried to lay out her case. "Look, she walked in with no appointment and demanded we stop everything and interview her for a non-existent position, Lonnie. Yes, I thought she was demanding Jamie's old job. Anybody would have thought so. There's no time to figure out things like this. Everyone is doing double duty around here the way it is."

"You have us on Fox as the media chumps of all time, then sit there and make excuses?" Lonnie took a deep breath. "Get somebody from HR into the act and do it now!" She snapped at the cowering Mallory. "How could you let it get this far?"

Mallory grabbed a house phone and spoke briefly. She brushed hair away and addressed the unwelcome visitor.

"Alright Miss Plain, you got your way. The interview is being set up now, twelfth floor, room 1250."

"Hmm." Hattie nodded. "Who?"

Mallory stopped. "Who what?"

"Who's gonna be doing the interviewing?"

Mallory stammered. "The, uh… I'm not sure."

Humphries spoke up. "Not me!"

"We'll find somebody!" Lonnie looked around. "See if Darryl Sykes has gone home yet."

Hattie laughed out loud. "Uh uh! Darryl Sykes is a fine boy but he can't make decisions about my future."

Mallory's heart was in her throat. Everyone in the room now knew her job was on the line. "Of course not, but he can recommend . . ."

Hattie cut her off. "Put me in front of James Pierce. If he doesn't want me, I'll go on home."

Lonnie stepped in. "You want to talk with James Pierce? There's no way. He's carrying the burden of our new format, and besides, he's travelling."

Mallory stood up and faced Hattie. "Actually Lonnie, *I* can do it."

Hattie couldn't suppress another loud laugh.

Lonnie rolled her eyes and pointed at Humphries. "Like it or not Mr. Humphries, it's your department!"

Hattie sat back down. "Miss Albrecht, maybe I didn't make myself clear. I'll *only* speak with Mr. James Pierce."

A man's voice came from the doorway. "That's good, cause he'll only talk with you."

There was silence as the stranger in an overcoat walked past an astonished Mallory and Lonnie Albrecht and stood before Hattie Plain. He smiled and extended his hand.

"James Pierce, Ms. Plain."

Chapter 14

Sunday August 8 1971
<u>The Black Liberation Action Command</u>
An Essay by Hattie Plain

Johnny Hughes, Ruthie Brown, Lovae Crowley and me, we took the bus to Central Park yesterday, figuring to take in the traveling American Civil Rights History display. But our attention was drawn to a small rally going on nearby. Thinking it was part of the program we just went on over to check it out. We were wrong. Signs planted in the grass called for a March on City Hall and a Take-Over by Any Means. Posters displayed the image of a fierce black man holding a machine gun with the red letters "BLAC".

"You can have what you can take!" Self-appointed General Hadis Victor of The Black Liberation Action Command prowled back and forth before the loose assembly. "There is no authority to stop you today!" The voice boomed out, followed by meager shouts of assent from the crowd.

"The white pigs and their black bootlickers wear badges and ride horses but they represent nothing!"

The speaker noticed us as we paused in the rear fringe. He pointed at Johnny.

"Say there brother, you that just joined us." The beret-wearing commander circled around toward him.

"When you march today, soldier, don't worry about nothing. Don't try and be safe, go ahead and be a target! They can only hurt your flesh; they don't own you anymore. Slavery's over, now it's time to fight back."

Ruth Brown stepped up. "You no-account thugs, don't you be using the language of decent men and martyrs to hide your wickedness."

A man with a huge Afro and sunglasses wearing a black jump suit with a red armband came and stood next to her.

"Careful now Jemima, you cuttin' it real close."

Ruth put her hands on her hips. "Who you callin' Jemima? You ain't nothing but a cartoon yourself."

Low laughter came from the sparse crowd. The angry general continued. "Hit them hard. Show no mercy." Then he drew an automatic handgun from his belt and waved it around. "Take their weapons! By the end of the day we will occupy their temple of power, we will control their fascist radio."

Well we had heard enough. Everybody knew there were radicals in every big city by then, kidnapping the rich, having shoot-outs with police. Here was another one. Johnny nodded to the general and we turned back toward the main display. But the guard stepped into our path.

Hadis motioned him to bring Johnny up front. I knew they were going to make an example out of this mild, friendly man. I'd seen intimidation before. The general smiled through his moustache and beard.

"Don't leave us without knowing us, unless you some kind of Tom." He taunted. "You a Tom, boy?"

Johnny turned and spoke quietly to the rude soldier.

"Excuse me now, my brother, I got business over there at the real civil rights display." The guard held him by an arm. Johnny pulled away. "Get off of me, man."

The general paced. "We're going to take you into the glory of a separate nation right here, brother. Self-government at hand, at last."

I had heard enough of this craziness. I slipped between Johnny and the guard. "Out of my way Paul Gerard, I known you since you was born and I knew your mama before that. You ain't nothing but a delivery driver. And not a very good one."

The general continued. "But the pigs don't want to lose their slaves, they're going to fight us. Can't any of us just walk away. This is your fight, brother it's time to sign up in the People's Force. I am Hadis Victor, your commander."

Commander?" Ruth yelled to the crowd, "You stole that costume from the movie people!" It drew more chuckles.

The speaker barked his orders. "Bring that Tom and that sister up to me!"

The small gathering turned and watched as the thug walked Johnny and me to the front. I held onto Johnny's hand and Lovae followed in her chair.

The self-appointed leader turned Johnny to face the crowd.

"There are millions of brothers and sisters armed with guns and grenades all over the land. Watching us here today. Waiting for the signal. What are we going to do, brothers, lie down? Walk away? What do you want, another 300 years of slavery? Join us right now. Stand up for your own!"

Johnny shook off the hold. "What do you know about slavery?"

I could see police barricades forming at the end of 97th Street, just before Broadway. This could easily become a tragedy and I felt duty-bound to stop it. I stepped forward and raised my arm. They must have thought it was a black power salute, because suddenly it got real quiet.

"Wait! Listen to me." I had some kind of natural authority that hour and intended to use it to steal this fool's thunder.

"This is not progress. This is pure hatred. This is the Klan in blackface. I have fought all my life for our place in this land. But I never signed up for this!"

"Wait? Ya'll hear that?" The general pulled me into center stage and laughed. "This woman wants you to wait?"

He put his hand on the back of my neck. "How long sister? How long you want me to wait before I own my own house, before I feed breakfast to the children, or educate them, before I run for President? Wait? For the white man to stop killing my brothers ten thousand miles away? Wait? For what? For the Klan to hand over the police departments? For good jobs? For simple justice? For respect? No brothers, the word wait is bad history. The new word is "Take!""

I was able to break free of his grip. Every eye was on me. I remember a fierce anger coming over me as I turned again to the assembly.

"Don't let this man hijack the progress we made in ten years, no, no that progress belongs to you, not him. Do what Dr. King says to do. Go demonstrate. Resist peacefully. Fill the jails. Vote! Change must come peacefully!"

The speaker took me by my hair and forced me to kneel. He uttered, "I'm in charge here, mammy. You all done."

I pulled away from him again. He raised his hand to smack me when Johnny stepped between us and stopped him. The guard spun Johnny around and punched him, first in the face then in the stomach. Johnny collapsed on the ground and covered up against the kicking.

I threw myself on Johnny and prayed out loud. That's when I saw a pistol, which had fallen from Hadis's waistband, laying right there in front of me, and I started to reach for it. But I got to my feet without it.

"Go on, there's your gun, General, shoot this old sister!"

I helped Johnny to stand. Lovae and Ruth joined hands and soon others became part of the circle. Lovae began singing, "We Shall Overcome", and soon we had a regular choir. Hadis waved his gun around and shouted more gibberish. I prayed he wouldn't start firing.

Then out of nowhere a squad of NYC Police surrounded the demonstration. The so-called general was disarmed and taken down. His assistant was forced to his knees and cuffed.

**

Hattie's face broke into a wide grin when she saw James Pierce. "Look at this! A black man in charge, now we're talkin'!"

Pierce offered a perfunctory smile. "Sorry to disappoint you so early Miss Plain, but the only color around here is green." He glanced at Breen and Lonnie. "I apologize for any inhospitality you may feel you received here today, and will gladly pay for any medical treatment made necessary by your visit."

Hattie sat back, saying nothing.

Pierce continued. "I will also write you a check for ten thousand dollars and supply a limo and an escort for your return trip home, if you will sign a simple release. Fair enough?"

Hattie searched his face. "Money's all you got? No thank you. I want something you don't have much of, Mr. Pierce. I want consideration, an honest interview."

The boss stopped. "For what?"

"Advice Columnist."

Pierce blinked away his surprise and looked around. "That's why you're here, stirring up all this negative publicity? You want a job?"

Hattie shot right back. "I came on down here for a job interview and there wasn't nobody willing to sit down and ask me one single question. Now then, interview me for real, and I'll go home on my own damn bus money."

Pierce, hands in pockets, still clad in his greatcoat, went quiet for a moment. Then he sat down, waving the others away.

"Fair enough. I'll grant you a ninety-minute interview, just the two of us, Miss Plain. What's said here stays here. You show me yours, I'll show you mine and at the end you Will walk out the front door peaceably. Then it's over forever. Do you agree?"

Hattie nodded. "I want a decision from you, before I leave."

"Done." Pierce lowered his voice. "And I want one thing from you." He pointed to the lobby where a throng of reporters were becoming impatient.

"Give those circling sharks out there a statement, and make this misunderstanding go away." He smiled. "I don't work well with a gun to my head."

"Me neither, Mr. Pierce." Hattie placed the heavy shopping bag in his lap. "Meanwhile you protect this."

Pierce felt the weight and made a face. "What's this?"

Hattie patted the bag. "My resume, sir. I came prepared."

Chapter 15

**

June 1975
To the Hattiesburg Chamber of Commerce

I am currently a charwoman in New York City. For three years however, I worked at a newspaper, The East Hattiesburg Caller. The publisher was an extraordinary ex-slave named Ponce Davis. He taught other freed slaves how to read then gave them the news they wanted and needed. In 1929 Mr. Davis was lynched and his newspaper torched. I saw it and fled. This marks the fiftieth anniversary of that night, and I think it's time to set the record straight. It was the Klan, led by Mr. J.J. Ketchum of Ketchum Hardware and Dry Goods that killed my aunt with his wagon on April 14, 1929. Then he hanged Ponce Davis. Later that night my family was murdered by Mr. Ferguson Thatcher. If either is alive you should have them arrested. I will return to Hattiesburg and testify against one or both.

This letter is prompted by a series of articles in the New York Times suggesting the 1974 Hattiesburg floods had uncovered a number of corpses with broken necks, the probable results of black lynching in the Hattiesburg area. I can no longer keep silent.

If the East Hattiesburg Caller is still publishing then give the publisher my regards and declare that Jefferson's Tree of Liberty was yet again refreshed on that Sunday afternoon fifty years ago with the sacred blood of that most decent American patriot and founder of the Caller, Mr. Ponce Davis, and other innocent citizens.

Yours Very Truly,
Hattie Plain, Honorary Mayor, 125th Street
Harlem New York

**

Pierce stood behind near the corridor, the Wal-Mart bag hanging from one hand as Hattie made her way across the marbled lobby. Humphries and Lonnie watched from the visitors' chairs, well away from the questioning theater. Mallory stood under a nearby ceiling lamp, her hair touched-up and make-up hastily reapplied.

A group of anxious reporters stood cloistered by the elevator door held in check by Potente and Breen. Potente instructed the reporters to keep a ten-foot perimeter from the subject.

As the old woman approached the mob of journalists, the questions poured out.

"Quiet, now!" Hattie shook her head and tapped her cane on the stone floor. "My name is Hattie Plain." She leaned on her cane and surveyed the assembly of reporters. "Look at you sorry people with nothing to report on. What you want here?"

Pierce smiled. This was textbook work. This old woman knew how to take control immediately.

"Who are you to them?" came a question from the pack.

"I'm a job applicant, honey. Who are you?"

An overweight man squeezed to the front, under-dressed in a sweatshirt and running pants. "Miss Plain, were you injured by the security people here at the newspaper?"

"Whoa, now!" Hattie frowned and banged her cane on the marble floor. "You ain't got a name?"

The reporter seemed at a loss for words. "Roland Proctor with The Village Voice. Miss Plain, why are you here? Are you injured?"

Before Hattie could speak another voice cut in. "Eve Saunders From the Times, Miss Plain. What exactly are you protesting? Have they dragged or beaten you?"

Hattie snorted a laugh, "What kind of . . ."

Another journalist broke in. "Tony Saenz, The Minority Reporter. Do you plan to sue these people for civil rights violations?"

A man with a microphone pushed his way forward. "Merle Pitt from the Around Town Radio Talk Show, Miss Plain . . ."

Hattie held up a hand, the voices quieted.

"The next one to interrupt an answer will be escorted out by this strong and capable guard Richard Potente. Now, what you fools talking about?" She paced before them, covering her purple wrists with the shawl. "Do I look all bruised and beaten to you?"

James Pierce glanced at Lonnie who was smiling broadly. This old woman's ability to work a crowd was fun to watch. He leaned forward to catch every word.

Hattie gestured to the executive staff huddled by the Admin Offices.

"Look here, these are good people, they publish a good newspaper. I came down here to interview for a job, and that's exactly what's about to happen. Now, I'm old and I fell, but these gentlemen helped me up and that's that. Ain't nothing to it. Y'all go on and find a real story."

"What kind of job are you interviewing for, Ms. Plain"?

Hattie stared at the nameless reporter who hadn't identified himself. "You tryin to get yourself thrown out?"

"No ma'am. Izzy Stottlemeyer, AP. What kind of job are you exactly looking to do?"

Advice Columnist of course."

"Second question… how old are you?"

"Next!"

A middle-aged woman raised her hand and got the nod from Hattie. "Eve Saunders, Ms. Plain, have you ever been arrested?"

Hattie leaned on her cane. Potente wheeled up an office chair and the retired charwoman sat in it. "Good Lord, woman', look at me, what do you think?"

Pierce moved over to Lonnie and Humphries. The personnel manager whispered loudly enough for everyone to hear.

"What idiot gave these vultures her rap sheet?"

Lonnie sighed. "I did."

Humphries coughed. "No offense, Ms. Albrecht. Highly illegal . . ."

"No kidding."

Pierce leaned forward and spoke in a low voice. "Well Lonnie, she's campaigning for the job right now, you know. Thanks to you."

Reporter Saunders spoke again. "You asked what do I think? Obviously, I can't speak for you, Miss Plain. Will you help me out?"

Hattie shook her cane. "How in the world do you think a black woman in America got anything accomplished these last 92 years without getting arrested?"

A voice rang out. "Ed Rumsfelt, UPI. Were you ever a prostitute?"

"I was arrested thirteen times. Various reasons. I had a boy headed for college and couldn't make the wages of a cleaning woman stretch far enough. What would you do? Marry a millionaire?"

"Ed Rumsfelt again, Miss Plain. What about the drugs?"

Hattie waved it away. "I had some pain, took some pills for it and got myself hooked. It passed."

"Tony Saenz. What can you tell us about your arrests in the sixties?"

Hattie smiled. "Martin told us to fill the jails, I and did. You thought all the racism was in the south?"

Lonnie shook her head slowly. "My God, James, she's playing them like a harp! It's beautiful!"

"Holding court." Pierce managed to keep a straight face. "They don't know what to do with her!"

Lonnie shook her head. "None of us do."

Pierce smiled. "We'll see."

An older man in a sweatshirt raised his hand. "Bernie Lachman, Evening Standard Miss Plain. Why do they call you the Mayor of 125th Street?"

Hattie thought for a moment. "Lived in the same apartment since 1930. Seen it all. Got to meet Mayor Koch on my 75th birthday, he gave me the Resolution."

Lachman grinned. "I knew him. What are your duties?"

Hattie leaned on her cane. "I look out every day from my front door and bless the whole street and everybody on it. If it's rainin', I use the window… provided the branches of my Hickory tree get trimmed up."

"Kyle Post, Newsday. Miss Plain, you had a son who…"

Hattie stood up. "I believe our question and answer time has run its course. I am happy we made acquaintance. God bless you all and please respect your jobs better."

The old celebrity turned and shuffled back to the admin offices.

Lonnie stepped forward. "Wait! Wait, please. Everybody. Please return the handouts I gave you."

No one paid attention. Lonnie approached Saenz, who was putting his notebook away. "Let's go Tony, give up the rap sheet."

"Source material Miss Albrecht. Sorry."

Pierce watched with concern as Lonnie herded Saenz And the others to a corner of the room and huddled for a few moments.

One by one they handed back Hattie's rap sheet, and then left.

"I'm impressed." Pierce took Lonnie aside. "How did you do that?

Lonnie was matter-of-fact. "I told them they were in possession of illegally obtained information, and everyone one of them and their newspapers would be held liable under the New York Privacy Act by Hattie Plain who has obvious access to City Hall as well as this newspaper if the material wasn't returned now."

"Good work." Pierce looked again at her quizzically. "What Privacy Act?"

Lonnie sighed. "Isn't there a Privacy Act somewhere, James?"

"Good bluff." Pierce replied. "But why would you admit to passing out illegal materials in the first place?"

"James," Lonnie became wistful. "This old woman is still going strong after ninety-two years of shooting straight, so maybe there's something to it!"

Pierce waxed curious. "What happened to you in the past fifteen minutes? Potente tells me you loathed this old lady, wanted to bust her for spying. Now you want to emulate her. Did I miss something?"

Lonnie massaged her forehead. "James, I was raised in a family that used this paper to keep out of hard decisions. As you know, they did and said things that served no purpose, until one day they got sick and handed me a broken metro. Without much notice."

The executive gaze went to the old woman.

"Frankly James, I really hadn't seen a good role model in the newspaper business until tonight, present company excepted." She touched his shoulder. "Let's get this sanitized. Excuse me."

Lonnie caught up with Hattie as she made her way to the interview room. She squeezed her hands.

"Miss Plain, I have misjudged you terribly. You're terrific. Whatever happens from here, bring those essays to us, we'll find a way to publish every one of them."

Hattie nodded. "Miss Albrecht, this is a fine newspaper."

"We're going to make it better."

Pierce touched Hattie on the sleeve. "This way Hattie Plain."

He slung the Wal-Mart bag across his shoulder and pointed to the Administration sign. "Let's find out exactly what brought you here today."

Chapter 16

Seated under the ceiling lights Pierce looked ferocious. His tall and wide forehead bore deep furrows, framing round and intense eyes. Cheekbones sat high on his face. His nose ran narrow then flared wide at the tip. His full mouth opened easily into a dazzling smile, but something told Hattie his wrath was equally quick. Short dreadlocks fell randomly hanging just above a gold earring. His custom suit contrasted well with his Mahogany complexion. He stacked up the notebooks and read the label on each.

Hattie pointed. "Each book is about twenty years of essays and such. My resume, sir."

"Your resume just got fatter, Miss Plain." He waved the printout. "This is your rap sheet, and as far as I'm concerned it's part of the record too. Fair enough?"

"Then you might as well start with my real name, Miriam Jones."

Pierce studied her. "Why'd you change it?"

**

April 14 1929.

An explosion in the Caller publishing building sent a fireball straight up past the tree line. It morphed into white fire, followed by a column of black smoke. Embers and sparks rained down on the shantytown of East Hattiesburg.

A terrified sixteen-year-old girl crouched behind a rain barrel clutching a metal can, watching in horror as the suspended body of Ponce Davis swung in the evening breeze, backlit by the flames.

Falling firebrands stung her flesh, hair and clothing. She jumped up to run but accidentally flipped the can, spilling coins and paper money onto the dirt street. She furiously scooped the money back into the coffee can, and then bolted across Forrest Street, past the courthouse.

She glanced back as she ran, certain she saw several of them pointing at her. She tore through the narrow dirt alleys behind the row of merchants and, without looking back again, cut through the Yellow Pine woods leading to Palmers Crossing.

Minutes later the exhausted teen raced past the hickory tree, crossed the wooden porch and burst into the two-room shack. Her hysterical panting and crying brought her mother running.

"What in the world…?" Oswega Jones took up the panicked teen in her arms.

"Mama's right here baby, what is it? Mr. Davis get mad at you about something? Good God girl, you all burned, I can smell it!"

Miriam could only get a few words out at a time. "Mama... they just hanged Mr. Davis... burned his building! I saw it, Mama... I saw them do it!" Miriam coughed and gagged. "And they saw me too, Mama."

Oswega stepped outside and saw the orange glow in the early evening sky. "Lord Jesus." She set the sixteen-year-old down and looked at the metal can with money in it.

"Did he give you this money, Precious?"

Miriam nodded, smearing away tears.

"Does anyone else know you got this money?"

Miriam shook her head no.

Oswega ran to the corner of the bedroom and grabbed a suitcase, which served as a study table. She laid it open on the mattress, then pulled Miriam's few blouses, dresses, stockings and underwear from the shelf, folding them into the open case.

Then with care she placed the framed family photograph, taken last year on Hattie's fifteenth birthday. She found a cloth bag and dumped the money into it, dirt and all.

Miriam looked out into the dusk. "Mama, where are we going?"

The mother listened to the night sounds and quickened the pace.

"Well honey, I got us a plan. It's real important you listen and do everything mama says, hear? Those men may come here and want to talk to us. If there's trouble I want you to take this suitcase and run to your Uncle Malcom's house. He's grieving over Sophie sure enough, but tell him he has to help you. It's less than a mile, you been there a thousand times. But tonight, you got to go the back way, cause you can't let them see you. Understand me?"

"Go?" Miriam began sobbing again. "Mama, I just got me a real newspaper job!"

"Shush now!" The mother shook her lightly. "You tell Malcom to take you to the train station in Clinton and use this money to buy you a ticket to New York City. Hear? That's where Uncle Alphonse lives; he'll take care of you for a bit."

She hugged Miriam and kissed her. "Come back here to East Hattiesburg when it's safe. You got that, baby? Now you take this suitcase; do as I say."

Miriam's voice trembled. "Please Mama let me stay here. I can hide."

"Honey, you . . ." Oswega's voice trailed off. They both heard the cacophony of horses and wagons turning onto the dirt road of their property. Miriam gripped on to her mother.

"Will you tell Papa all about it when you see him?"

Oswega held her tears. "Of course, baby. Now, go. Don't let nobody see you, hear? Remember your mama and daddy love you."

Frightened and exhausted Miriam slipped out the back door and scrambled up the small hill, making a hiding place behind a bush close to a rock outcropping. Beside her the trail of pine needles led to her Uncle's cabin.

Suddenly a dozen men with horses and a wagon pulled up to her house. In the fading light she recognized her father Rupert, sitting in the wagon bed.

An armed man jumped off his horse and stood before the shack. "Alright, woman, come on out now. We gotta talk some."

Hattie recognized the man as Ferguson Thatcher, the Deputy Sheriff. A man in the wagon made her father stand up. Her heart leapt when she saw him bound hand and foot. A noose sat loosely around his neck.

Oswega came out to the porch. "What you want?"

"Well, we need your little pickaninny out here. She was playin' with fire in that printing plant, why now the whole town is about burned up real good."

"Miriam ain't home yet."

On Thatcher's signal two men brushed past Oswega and entered the house with lit lanterns. They emerged a minute later empty handed.

Thatcher came closer. "Now don't you know, these fellas are mighty upset cause the fire your little girl set, why it liked to burn up everything." He re-cradled the shotgun. "Best you send her on out now."

"I told you she ain't back from her job yet."

The horse was led so that the wagon sat directly under a large branch of the Hickory. Somebody tossed the rope up to a boy in the tree who draped it over the high branch. He hauled on it until Rupert's head jerked up. Then he wrapped the rope around a lower branch before tying it off.

"Now then, woman," continued Thatcher, "It's come down to this. You send out the girl from wherever you got her hid, and we'll send in your husband." He spat tobacco. "We ain't gonna hurt the girl- just want to talk with her. But your man, well he might get hurt if you don't cooperate. You got one minute."

Her mother disappeared for a moment, and then reappeared at the door, clutching her apron slightly differently.

Miriam remembered the butcher knife on the cutting board near the door. One thing was clear. Mother was buying the whole minute so Miriam could get further away. But Miriam couldn't run, the bush and rock were in plain view under the strong moonlight. She picked up a Hickory nut and worked it nervously with her fingers.

"Alright then." Thatcher gave a hand signal.

A loud slap and shrill "hee-ya" launched the horse forward, and Rupert was jerked off the back of the wagon. He swung from his neck, kicking and struggling.

Miriam stared uncomprehendingly as Oswega raced past Thatcher to the tied-off rope and began hacking at it with the butcher knife.

Thatcher fired twice and she was blown backwards, collapsing under Rupert's gasping form.

The deputy pointed to the shack. "Burn it. Check the roads in and out boys, without money or clothes, this one ain't going too far tonight."

Miriam Jones took off running when the shots rang out. Looking over her shoulder she could again see the glow of fire and the river of sparks going up into the sky. Her family was gone and every trace of her existence in East Hattiesburg wiped out. Nothing remained but a plan to get to New York.

She ran to Uncle Malcom's house.

April 15 1929.

There are times I think about Mr. Davis and I feel troubled down to my soul. He lived and died witnessing the glory of a people struggling into the light. I'm that witness now. I'm on a northbound train headed to a new life, and all I got is my name, a suitcase full of clothes and a few paper dollars. And a family photograph. The money will get spent, the suitcase will fall apart, and the clothes will wear out. The picture will fade. But my name is my nature, planted mightily in the soil of hope and I know it will survive, and become a tree, robust enough for children to climb and birds to nest. And strong enough to withstand the storms.

Chapter 17

**

James Pierce looked away and blew his nose. This was more than he expected.

"So Miriam Jones got out?"

Hattie nodded and dabbed her eyes. "She got to the house all right. Her Uncle Malcom repacked Miriam's suitcase with Sophie's clothes and such, then took her by mule the eight miles to Clinton. He told her he was leavin' for Chicago, that it was too dangerous to stay in Hattiesburg. That's when she realized everything was truly gonna have to change whether she liked it or not."

Pierce watched Hattie's face transform from fear to peace. He leaned in and touched her hand. "New town, new start . . . new name?"

The visitor nodded vigorously.

"I had to stop callin' myself Miriam Jones and come up with somethin' new. Didn't know how far the Klan might reach out, you see, and New York was still a long way off. Well, the first name took care of itself, being as I was from Hattiesburg. And Bessie Coleman was a pilot of an airplane, so I just changed the spelling. Hattie Plain. But the trip north on a slow train was dangerous for a teenage girl by any name."

Pierce was buried in the first volume. He looked up. "You went the 1300 miles alone?"

"Oh, I made me a friend right off." Hattie shook her head. "Man sat down next to me and we talked a long time. He saw me eatin' crackers and offered to treat me to a real fine chicken dinner out at a real restaurant, him and a friend of his he planned to meet up with in Knoxville Tennessee."

Pierce made a face. "Doesn't sound too promising."

Hattie waved her hand. "Oh, he was an evil man, and his friend was just as bad. It wasn't no restaurant either, it was a whorehouse and speakeasy. Prohibition you know." Pierce read the pain in her eyes as Hattie spoke slowly.

"They knocked me out and took my clothes off and had their way with me in a little room. Later on that night the score got settled." She sat back. "Yes sir."

"'Score got settled'…" Pierce rapidly scrutinized her arrest record on the background report. "Two Tennessee men killed." He looked up. "How much of this can I know?"

"Those men died that night, I ain't sayin' how."

The cleaning lady gazed out Pierce's window into the electrified New York night. The rain had washed the streets and the buildings and left the air clean.

Hattie continued. "You know the next train wasn't due till the next afternoon, so I walked back the four miles to the station and slept on a bench seat. "Got woke up by the Sheriff who hauled me to the jail for two days, tried his best to make me confess to the murders of those two at the river."

Pierce puckered his brow. "White southern Sheriff, nineteen twenty-nine, I'm surprised they didn't get a confession from you. The hard way."

"What? That fat old white man threatening me? What could he possibly take from me at that point?" She chortled. "First time I used the name Hattie Plain legally was right there in that old jail."

Pierce rubbed his temples. "Hattie, if you murdered two men, you should know there's no statute on that."

Hattie grunted. "I didn't say I killed anybody. But there is justice, Mr. Pierce. That can't be stopped."

"Enough with the homilies!" Pierce seared her with his disapproving look. "If you killed them just don't admit it to me."

She waved her hand at the office. "What's said here stays here. Was that *you* said that?"

He sighed. "It could make me an accessory after the fact, just being cautious."

"Hm huh. You thinkin' like a lawyer, but you supposed to be publishing to the people. Tell me Mr. Pierce, what you think a child might do if she's watched her parents and her benefactor murdered, house burned down, job taken away, dreams destroyed, then she's raped and beaten, tricked and betrayed, *before* she has any physical, emotional or natural defenses, and *all* in a lawless community run by her worst enemies." Hattie brightened up. "Then suddenly right there in deepest trouble, she finds a means of payback. Mr. Pierce, this ever happened to you?"

"Of course not."

"I rest my case."

"Yes, but it reeks of revenge and base instinct." Pierce Raised an eyebrow. "Hardly the bedrock for a competent advice column."

"Well, bad things have happened to your readers and revenge might cross their minds. What you gonna tell them? 'Sorry lady but the Advice Columnist has no idea what you're talking about?'"

Pierce read on. "Okay. According to your sheet, you were arrested for being a public nuisance in April of that year, yes?"

"I was pregnant from one of those two men. But I didn't know it yet. When I got to New York, there wasn't anybody could help me find this Uncle Alphonse I was supposed to meet. Mama never had the chance to write him about me."

"How'd you get by?"

"Oh, I stayed in the Grand Central Station, sleeping and using their bathrooms. After two weeks the police picked me up and booked me for being a nuisance. At least in jail I got some food and the clerk lady was nice to me. I stayed there for a whole month. She sent me to a doctor friend of hers and he told me I was pregnant. He arranged for me to stay in a community center for pregnant young women without husbands, where I learned how to mop the professional way."

Pierce nodded. "Basic training…"

"That's right. After a while I got me a job cleaning toilets and hallways at the Times Building. But I knew my real calling was newspaper writing so I found out the name of an editor at the Times and dropped him a letter."

August 1929

Dear Mr. Lewis, As Managing Editor of the New York Times you are in a perfect position to see and report the past, present, and now, the future! Because here I am, looking <u>with</u> you, young and optimistic, pointing to a new day with new inventions and new people, describing how all of us pulling on the oars at the same time, can make that boat move right along! That's my beat, those are my people! I'm Hattie Plain and I work in your building as a cleaning woman, but if you only knew my heart, you'd see right away it is newspaper reporting that it craves. I see black, white, and color, young, old, and in-between. I hear the voice of that new world saying come; bring your gifts into the house! Well here I am Mr. Lewis. Here I am right now, gift in hand, ready to carry on the tradition of your great newspaper in the language of people you may not have met. Yet.

Hattie Plain

"Imagine the excitement I felt!" Hattie sat forward. "Man had me come in and he read my essays. Promised me that I could come back in the summertime to speak with

the Features Editor, if I still wanted to work for the Times."
Hattie laughed. "*If?* Ha! I told him I'd clean bathrooms for
fifty years if that's what it took to get that Features job!"

Pierce smiled sadly. "Let me guess, that's what it
took…"

"Um hum. And never got the job! You see Mr. Pierce,
by December the economy was getting bad and we all
knew the game had changed. I had the baby in January.
That's when I met Reverend Cecil Addison and his wife
Clara. I was livin' in a shed behind the doctor's house."

**

January 1930

Hattie looked up from feeding the baby. A heavy
woman dressed in fine clothes and a wide green hat
darkened the door.

"Miss Plain, I'm Clara Addison, wife of Reverend
Cecil Addison. May I come in?"

"Yes ma'am."

She entered cautiously, examining the sparse quarters.

"You have a new baby according to Dr. Jefferson. He
and my husband serve on the board of the Center where
you've been staying. He says you're an extraordinarily
grown-up girl for being so young. And he says you got no
place to go in New York?"

Hattie held the baby and rocked from side to side.

"Yes ma'am."

"And are you planning to get back to work after a bit?"

Hattie nodded.

"Well, we have an extra room in our house. You can stay there for a small stipend if you'll help cook and clean. I'll take care of the baby while you work at your job."

"Hattie grinned from ear to ear. "Yes ma'am!"

**

Pierce poured coffee which Hattie declined.

"So you had a job and a safe place to live. Not a bad start."

"Ain't said a word!" Hattie sighed. "The situation with the Preacher Addison and his wife was a Godsend. I even had a place to grow the Hickory Nut I'd taken from Mississippi. Sprouted right there in the window.

"But over time Addison pushed his wife out of the picture and took control of the relationship with me. He raised my room and board stipend until I had to hand him almost everything I made except bus fare. And I still had to clean.

"And he'd take me into his study and preach half the night. I was so tired; always falling asleep, hardly saw my baby. Somctimes he'd get right up on me." Hattie shivered.

Pierce nodded. "So, Preacher Addison had some non-spiritual ideas about you and him?"

"He hugged me all the time, said I was like a daughter. But his hugs happened too often, lasted too long, and were becoming . . . intimate. Especially when Mrs. Addison wasn't around. Kisses made their way to my mouth, and I knew damn well there wasn't gonna be any escape for me right soon.

"I stayed out of his way for a while. I hid two dollars a week for four months. I told some people I was in the market for an apartment to share, I even posted a note on the workers' bulletin board."

"So, you made a plan. Good."

"Not that easy, Mr. Pierce. Preacher Addison heard about me wanting to move out, and he came to me one night, said he felt betrayed. Said that I was his daughter slappin' him in the face for all the good he'd done me, and on and on. I tried to explain that this was just natural; I was almost seventeen years old and it was time to get on my own. But he said the baby wouldn't be safe with me out there in the devil's world, and that he'd keep the baby there in his house until I changed my mind."

"Good God." Pierce sighed. "You shoot him too?"

"You got any children yourself Mr. Pierce?"

"No. Sorry." Pierce shifted uncomfortably. "So, what did you do?"

"I took the baby to work with me next day, told the preacher's wife I was going to the doctor. I couldn't go back there, had to leave all my clothes and such, but there was no other place for me. I remember working all day with that child slung across my back and a Hickory sprout in my pocket. And nobody said nothing to me.

"Then around four o'clock in the afternoon I went to the broom closet where there's some peace and quiet, and

I got down on my knees and I prayed to Jesus himself to show me the answer." Hattie smiled at the ceiling. "You know, it only took Him twenty-four hours."

Chapter 18

**

May 30 1930, Friday afternoon

Hattie waited at the service elevator with her mop, bucket and sleeping baby. Pauline Law passed her with a cart and broom.

"Say girl, you still looking for a room to rent?"

The teenage Hattie almost jumped. "What you got?"

"Well, I seen a sign from the bus, corner of 125th and Lexington. 'Room for Rent,' it said. Arrow pointed down 125th Street. Lots of Colored movin' in there now."

Hattie threw a hug around Pauline's neck.

It was early in the evening when Hattie got off the bus at the designated corner and found the sign. 125th Street was lined with youthful Maples and rows of identical apartment buildings. The narrow apartments were sturdy and clean, each offering a patch of lawn. Hattie found the address and climbed the steps of the walk-up, the baby slung on her back. At the door she pressed a bell. A disembodied voice startled her. "Who is it?"

The teenager didn't know where to look. Finally she blurted out her name. "Hattie Plain."

The voice squawked again. "What you want, Hattie Plain?"

"Looking to rent a room."

In a minute the heavy front door swung open. A woman in her mid-twenties with shiny straight hair and wearing a satin dress leaned in the doorway. A cigarette stuck out of her lipstick mouth.

Hattie spoke first. "You got a room to rent out like the sign says?"

The woman started to shut the door.

"Wait now!" Hattie smiled. "Answer. Unless you a mute. You a mute?"

The cigarette came out. "Am I a what?"

"Mutes can't talk but I see you hear me just fine, so I'm already wrong."

The woman rolled her eyes. "I see, you hear…you're a million laughs. You eighteen yet?"

The sixteen-year-old drew herself up. "Count on that."

"Yeah and you impressing me right outta my drawers, honey. Bye."

"Wait!" Hattie pushed back against the closing door. "I need this place."

The woman glanced at the flyer in the grip of Hattie's hand.

"That sign say anything about a baby?"

Hattie thought quickly. "Well this baby is quiet. Sleeps all day and all night 'cept when I feed her."

The lady whispered loudly. "I got too many babies come by here the way it is. Except they don't ever sleep and all they do is eat. Keep looking, sister."

Hattie stood her ground. "Sounds like I need to write a column about those babies."

"Column?" The woman in the door snorted a laugh. "You got some kind of real job?"

"Yes indeed!" Hattie beamed. "I work at the New York Times."

She looked Hattie over. "Doing what?"

"Cleaning bathrooms and halls, first ten floors. It's what I do for now, but that's all gonna change. I'm really a journalist."

"Yeah and I'm really Bessie Smith."

"Who?"

"Never mind. At least you working." She held the door open. "I'm Edith Plummer Crowley. When's the last time you and your baby ate?"

The two women went into Edith's flat. Hattie had never seen anything so spacious. Or that messy. The kitchen sink was piled high with pots and plates. Clothes were strewn on the floor and furniture. Saucers and ashtrays were full of cigarette butts. Empty gin bottles filled a corner of the kitchen.

Edith made baloney sandwiches and the two women toured the messy unit.

"You get one bedroom, one bathroom," recited the landlord. "Don't waste hot water. Three months, then I decide if you stay. Keep that baby under control, we be all right." She motioned toward the kitchen. "You can cook all you want, long as you buy your own food. Vegetable man comes through twice a week.

The landlady held out her hand. "Two people, that's forty a month. In advance."

Hattie winced. "Forty dollars every month..."

"Money talks." Edith opened the door. "You know what walks."

Hattie stopped and reached for her purse.

"I have thirty! Plus, I can clean up this place and keep it nice."

Edith calculated. "Thirty, and you clean? Alright, dishes, dust, mop, wash, make beds."

"Beds? I look like a maid to you?" Hattie looked around again. "I'll clean so there's no dust, sweep floors. Windows once a month. Plus empty ashtrays."

Edith pointed to the sink. "And dishes. I hate dishes."

Hattie thought. "Okay, twenty-five and dishes. Twenty-two, and I wash your clothes. I'll even plant vegetables in the weed patch out front, and a Pignut Hickory Tree too."

"Tree would look good, baby." Edith laughed. "Look here, I got musicians comin' over all the time, poets, junkies, rabble-rousers, honey this place is Grand Central with a horn. You and that baby just have to sleep through it."

Hattie shelled out twenty-two dollars. "Gonna be fine for me and my baby."

"What's this child's name?"

"No name."

Edith looked at Hattie quizzically. "No name? If I ever have a baby he's gonna have a name."

"That's your business."

"Well you get busy making it look good Hattie Plain, cause like I said, they's a group of no-goods comin' tonight and we're gonna make some noise. But I want it clean so's they're not as apt to abuse the place quite as much."

"What kind of noise do you make, Edith Crowley?"

"I'm a singer, child."

"Gospel?"

"No baby, blues and jazz. Most of my gigs are here in Harlem but I'm startin' to get work all over New York. Say, you ever hear of Bill Ellington?"

Hattie shook her head.

"He's movin' up fast too… looks like I'm gonna tour with that cat. They call him Duke, you know."

"That's real good." Hattie smiled. "When you gonna change your name?"

Edith stopped. "Change my name? Why in the world…"

Hattie shrugged. "Girl has to change her name if she's going to the top. Otherwise her past might reach right out and hold her back."

The singer laughed. "Yeah? And what's my name gotta be to hit the top?"

Hattie remembered the bus ride past the Savoy Grille, and the jewelry store where the bus waited at a stop sign. It read Richard Bobbi's Fine Watches. Hattie looked straight at her new landlady. "Bobbi."

Crowley nodded. "Bobbi's all right. Bobbi What?"

The teenager grinned, remembering the diner's white neon script scrawled across the blue-mirrored background.

"Savoy!" she said eagerly. "Bobbi Savoy."

"Bobbi Savoy? Ooo, I like that!"

Edith grabbed a floor lamp, drew it close to her mouth.

"Ladies and gentlemen, Miss Bobbi Savoy!" She turned to Hattie, her face lit up. "Oh yeah! Watch out world, Bobbi Savoy is here!"

Chapter 19

**

"Let me get this straight, Hattie Plain." The executive began pacing a small circle, scratching his back with a letter opener. "You gonna sit there and tell me you gave Bobbi Savoy her name?"

Hattie smiled. "Mmm hmm. I surely did."

Pierce threw his head back. "Amazing!" For a moment he was a teenager again. "I grew up listening to her albums, all scratchy and beat up. Ha. Made her more exotic in a way!"

"Oh, she was scratchy and beat-up in life too, Mr. Pierce."

Pierce quickly composed himself. "Well. Harlem in 1930, and you right there. You must have seen some history, woman."

Hattie nodded enthusiastically. "Mr. Pierce, try to imagine what a teen-age girl from Mississippi feels like in the same room with W.E.B. Dubois and Langston Hughes, Duke Ellington and Thelonious Monk. Aw, I met jazzmen, poets, politicians and novelists. Baby-sat for Louis Armstrong."

"That was history being made, sister."

"I taught Art Blakely to read when he was twelve years old. Delivered Charlie Parker's horn to the Tuxedo Club once and the Cotton Club twice."

Sitting back with closed eyes, Hattie's reverie continued.

"Um um, that man was in a daze I'm telling you."

Pierce sat on the desk. "So the apartment on 125th became a flash point for the whole thirties Harlem Renaissance. Fascinating!"

"And Bobbi was the center of it. Oh, they buzzed around her, the entire thing was unstoppable. I was witnessing something and didn't have a clue of its true importance."

Pierce glowed. "I studied these leaders in school, Miss Plain. Dubois was an educator and quite the radical at the time. Took an edge that George Washington Carver never endorsed, you know. Hughes was a writer and poet, and a major rebirth voice too.

"And the musicians!" Pierce waxed excited again. "I've always wondered, what was the fuel in that cultural explosion—music or political thought? Or both?"

Hattie closed her eyes. "It was just human brotherhood, man. The cats refused to be kept down. They found a way to deliver their own voice. Nobody knew this was history being made. Nobody set out to introduce the new yeast into the white dough. It just happened. They just blossomed like a fruit tree by the river." Hattie nodded with a self-conscious grin. "And they trusted me for some reason, Mr.

Pierce. Talked to me endlessly, drunk and sober, high and clean, joyful and tearful, about everything in their world. We were all just tryin' to figure it out!" Hattie broke out laughing. "This was my new family, Mr. Pierce!"

**

May 1931

By ten a.m. the living room had thinned out. Bobbi was draped across a stuffed chair, snoring. Ellington and his three musicians had come and gone, leaving the booking agent Speed Garron, and young musician Jamal Handler.

Handler was propped in the corner playing the sax softly. The bearded agent stumbled to the kitchen and poured cold coffee. Hattie washed glasses at the sink.

"Hattie, Harlem is almost all Negro now." Garron stood next to her. "A year from now we'll be able to drop the word 'almost'. The Cotton Club is changing, and we need Negro acts and lots of them. Now, you see a lot of entertainers come and go in this place, who's fresh on the scene I need to know about?"

Hattie thought. "Most of the young cats I see belong to Duke or Shaw or Lester Young." She paused to listen to the easy sax flowing from the other room. "Now there's a good sound right there. Brings to mind Coleman Hawkins."

"What sound? Who you talking about?"

"Listen to that gentle horn. He's Jamal Handler and that's him in the next room."

Garron went to the archway.

"Him? I thought he was with Ellington."

Hattie stood beside him, gazing at the young musician. "No no, he's playing with Fletcher Henderson right now at Small's Paradise but he ain't signed, and I believe he's looking to put his own band together."

Jamal Handler lowered the musical axe. "Y'all talking about me?"

Hattie went back to the sink. "You want cold coffee too?"

Jamal got up and wandered into the kitchen. Garron noticed the attraction between them. Handler moved up behind Hattie as she washed up the pots and pans. She spun around with a skillet in hand.

"Don't be sneakin' up like that."

Handler took the pot and poured the dregs into an old cup. He leaned closer.

"Hattie, you sweet on anybody?"

Garron stepped up. "So, Jamal, you with Fletcher Henderson?"

Jamal was modest. "Fill-in, s'all."

Hattie turned her head. "What kind of question is that?"

Speed held up his hands. "Hey, I'm only trying to talk with this man about his career in music."

Hattie glanced at her admirer. "No, I mean this 'sweet on somebody' talk. What is that about?"

"You got a man, Hattie?" Handler began to massage her neck.

Hattie lifted the skillet. "I got this to lay upside your head, that's what I got."

The white man stepped in with an outstretched hand. "We didn't get introduced. I'm Speed Garron, I book acts into the Cotton Club. I also work with Connie's, Tuxedo and a few new clubs getting started."

He watched Jamal's face for signs of interest. "There's a renaissance going on right here Jamal, so I urge all you young musicians to get into the boat! Keep working that axe, I can get you booked."

"Yeah?" Jamal pointed to his own chest while gazing at Hattie. "There's a renaissance going on in here too."

Hattie dried her hands. "What you asking me?"

"If you tied up with somebody." The young man stroked her cheek. "If not, I'm gonna be the man in your life."

"Ha!" Hattie hung out the wash rag. "I got no time for men. Got me a child in the next room." She turned to conceal her delight. "You an axman talking sweet to me while this town is movin' like it is? First, you put that band together and book yourself into this man's club, then you come sniffin' around me."

Garron spoke up. "Look, Jamal. I heard you wailing in there and you're exactly what I'm looking for. Come in here."

The two men walked into the living room and sat down.

"Jamal, you want your own band? Well I got a piano player, guitarist and a drummer available. I know where there's a bass man, and a trumpet just coming off tour. Interested?"

"Oh yeah." Jamal Handler wore a white tank top undershirt. "Look here, I'm twenty-two already Mr. Garron, I gotta do this now before I get too old."

He reached to set down the coffee down and Garron saw the needle scars.

"Hold up there, hoss. I don't work with junkies, might as well be up front with you."

"I ain't a dope addict." The musician shook his head. "Not any more, anyway. Don't drink too much and don't smoke cigs or chew tobacco."

He smiled and looked toward Hattie, leaning against the wall.

"Trying to cut down on cigars and women too."

Garron looked up at the teen. "Yeah well you mess with that woman and you'll be a tea-totaling Sunday school teacher in a year."

Handler smiled. "Ain't all bad. She'd raise up a child right."

"I known you for ten minutes, Jamal Handler." Hattie began dusting the room. "What you know about me?"

Jamal walked to the window where two birds chased each other continuously in the branches of the sapling Hickory. The musician watched in fascination.

"Can't tell if the female wants this cat or not."

Garron observed the courtship. "Lady bird making sure that only the serious players get into the game. No walk-ons."

Hattie turned to Jamal. "Look man, you got to find out something about me. I got me some past, you know. There's talk, and sooner or later you gonna hear it."

Jamal glanced down at his arm. "Well Hattie, you gotta take people the way they are today." He watched the fluttering birds, then looked at the fat booking agent. "Don't know about you Mr. Garron, but outside these two birds, ain't nobody I know can be looked at real close up."

Chapter 20

**

Pierce sat back and studied the rap sheet. "So, when did the baby die?"

The question came like a slap in the face. But Hattie hadn't forgotten Pierce was a newspaperman first.

"Nineteen thirty-two, July. Baby quit breathing one night. Went to the hospital but they couldn't do nothing. Dead. No explanation."

Pierce tried draining the empty coffee cup. "A baby with no name, which you didn't really want, dies for no reason. Do you really accept that at face value?"

Hattie folded her arms. "I accept he knew he was in the wrong place at the wrong time and chose to check out one night. He had no name because I don't know which man the father was. Names are important, Mr. Pierce, you don't just hand out names like they was worthless old leaves."

"I agree." He looked up at her. "Everybody is entitled to a name. So, what did you do?"

"I was depressed, stayed low for a year or so. Got myself a little further into the dark side of the Harlem cultural scene."

"Meaning what exactly?"

"Started drinkin'. Used marijuana a lot. Experimented with heroin. Memories were creeping in more and more, bringing the pain. Funny, when a terrible thing happens, you first just deal with it. You remember it a certain way."

Pierce nodded. "Got to get past it."

"That's the hard part." Hattie sat back. "If you ain't careful, later on you enshrine it. Then you medicate it. Then you die from it." Hattie waved the notebook. "For the first time I could cancel that pain right here right now, you know what I'm saying? Don't make it right of course. But it was all I had."

"So you became a player out of self-pity?"

Hattie fanned herself with paper. "*It* came *to* me. The whole building got overtaken by the faster element of Harlem, you know what I mean. I managed to keep Bobbi on time for her appointments, now that was a big job. She was using dope every day and missing rehearsals. Couldn't talk right half the time. I wound up arranging things with her dealers."

"You facilitated her addiction?"

"Worse. I started arranging everything, call girls for the fellas, bootleg whiskey shipments, whatever the traffic was. And the gamblers! I became the housemother, ran girls, dealt drugs, I was even a lookout for police on Saturday nights. But I didn't prostitute myself, didn't need to. I picked my men, they didn't pick me. But they all came to me for advice."

Pierce looked through the paperwork. "Where was Jamal during that time?"

"He stayed in California a few years. Wrote me every so often."

October 1934

My Dear Hattie

This is the second year of touring and I got to say things are going real good out here on the road for us. But there's some bad problems out here for people, terrible dust storms blowing the land clear away. People are moving west mostly California, just walking away from their farms. There's clubs in Los Angeles where white people mix with colored, dance together right on the floor. It's a wide-open place! We should look at moving out there when the time is right. Anyway we're in Kansas City this week. Back to the coast next month. Nobody ever heard of the Jamal Handler Orchestra before, but we sure are packing the house. The bus broke down again, and last week we couldn't find a hotel that could take the whole band, so we wound up all scattered around. Speed stays with us even though there's fine white hotels and restaurants everywhere. I think about you all the time. These women in the clubs are glamorous and on the lookout for musicians, but they don't come near being the kind of woman I'm looking for. Only you do that for me.

Your man Jamal

Pierce read more. "You didn't leave your job at the Times?"

"Umm uh, I sure didn't." Hattie looked into the night. "Never did believe my new sinful life would last too long."

"So, when did you actually break with that lifestyle? And why?"

"You sure are one curious man, Mr. Pierce."

"Rules of engagement we both agreed to, Miss Plain. Just let me know when you think we're all done."

"Oh that's all fine. I got nothing to hide." Hattie smiled. "Fact is, prohibition got repealed and I couldn't give that bad hooch away."

"But it was more than that wasn't it?" Pierce was tracing a line with a pen. He looked up. "You went a little crazy one night, no?"

"Oh well, you readin' ahead a bit." Hattie unclipped her hat and used it to fan herself. "It was Christmas night 1935 and my Lord I was feelin' awful. Everybody had gone their way, partying was over. Bobbi was touring in the West. I was alone sittin' in the stairwell. I don't know if I was dreamin' or just what, but I saw a hand writing something on the wall, traveling toward me slow like a creeping shadow."

Pierce looked up. "DTs maybe?"

"Naw, honey, I just knew it was death stalking me. Then I saw the ghosts of Mr. Davis and both my parents, and those two men in Tennessee and my little dead baby, all comin at me trying to warn me about something."

"Warn you? About what?"

"That I had gone to a far country and sold myself for nothin'. That I was just as dead they were. Maybe more. I sat there shaking, began to realize what awful things I had seen and done. The slaughter of my parents. The lynching of the most decent man ever set foot on this earth. My cold-blooded assassination of two misguided men. Yeah, that was a big one. The ghosts entered into me and made me crazy."

Hattie stumbled on the word and wiped her eyes. Pierce leaned forward with a Kleenex box.

She continued softly. "I ran like a mad woman naked into the street warning everybody that the end was here."

Pierce stared at his companion. The low light emphasized her aged face and hooded eyes. It wasn't difficult to imagine this woman on an inebriated rant.

"Did you sleep it off?

"I wasn't just drunk, James Pierce! I'd lost my mind completely. By morning I was strapped to a gurney, and taken to the New York State Hospital insane asylum. Spent an eternity in that wretched hole! I was raped, I stunk, I starved, couldn't get anybody's help. Thirty days later they let me out."

Pierce fumbled through the pages. "You were okay by then?"

"Oh, I got through it but I found myself confused about almost everything. By the time my birthday rolled around in 1936, I'd officially lived an entire lifetime in twenty-three years and couldn't tell you right from wrong anymore."

Hattie slipped the family portrait out of the bag and handed it to Pierce.

"That afternoon I got this photograph out that my mother had packed that awful night in Hattiesburg. I was fifteen years old when it was taken."

Pierce held it for maximum light. "Quite beautiful."

Hattie leaned forward. "Most people said I was pretty as any girl in Mississippi. The world was my oyster, they said."

Hattie traced her finger over the picture. "These two others, well they sacrificed their actual lives so that this pretty girl would have a chance at the oyster, you know? A chance to be Bessie Coleman or Bessie Smith. Or Hattie Plain!"

"So, you began to see yourself as the product of sacrifice?"

"Not only my parents but Mr. Davis, too! God spoke to Me right there and then, and I knew I was all done being the devil's pincushion, you know? I would do the right thing, at all times and in all ways. I was gonna make my parents, my dead baby, and especially Mr. Davis all proud. Plus, I'd be alright with my own self too."

James Pierce looked over the paperwork spread out before him.

"After thirty days and the physical torture you endured, well, you had to have lost your job at the Times. . ."

The visitor rummaged through the second book of Essays on Life. "Well I got a pink slip sent to me after one week of missing work. But when I got out of the hospital there was another letter sittin' right there waitin' to be read."

**

May 1 1936

Hattie rode the elevator up from the Times lobby. The operator barked "fourth floor!" and opened the gates. Hattie re-read the letter and managed to locate the Office of Building Maintenance Personnel.

Inside, the typists and file clerks didn't look up. A man with a toupee behind the counter stepped over and scanned the underweight girl. Her eye was still swollen and a tooth was chipped, noticeable when she smiled.

"Do you have an appointment?"

Hattie displayed the letter.

"Ah yes." He shuffled over to the office and motioned for her to precede him. He closed the door and Hattie found herself in an ante room. She took a seat.

"Wait here," he croaked, taking the letter from her hands.

Time passed. Hattie nodded off in the chair and was suddenly awakened by the opening of the door. A man in a pinstriped suit stood next to her chair.

"Miss Plain?"

She jumped up. "I'm Hattie Plain."

"Miss Plain, please be seated. I am Phillip Boethe, Operations Manager for this newspaper." He sat beside her. "I don't know you, or the events that have happened to you, but I am here to help you. First, you haven't lost your job." He handed her an envelope. "This is pay for the month you were absent. Now, you have an appointment this afternoon with the company doctor and dentist. You're to take two weeks off for medical rehabilitation, paid by the Times, and return to a senior level custodial position. I don't know who is looking out for you Miss Plain, but I welcome you back to our family."

**

James Pierce smiled. "So, a stealth benefactor came into play? I'm glad. You needed some luck after all you'd been through."

"Luck? Look here, Mr. Pierce; you make your own luck. What happened to me had nothing to do with luck. There is justice, Mr. Pierce, indeed there is, and it works its way into our lives whether we like it or not."

"All right, all right." Pierce wagged his head. "So, what happened to your roommate while you were in the tank?"

"Well I got back in time to see what true pain looked like."

"And it looked like Bobbi Savoy, right?"

"This crazy girl was so hard into drugs at the same time she was becoming a blues-singing legend. You see, she was part white, part confused, part angry and part greedy."

Pierce stared at the wall. "Yes, I read her bio. Abandoned as a baby, and a lot of early on raping' by an uncle. A prostitute by age 12."

Hattie nodded. "Mr. Pierce, nobody could change that woman, she wasn't gonna give up those drugs for nothing, you know. Just tryin' to get her on her feet, and to the club was a chore. Now, on stage singin', that was different. She was all right then. Oh we all wanted to help her, but everybody in that scene was a mess. I especially owed her, man, cause she took me and the baby off the streets a few years earlier." Hattie rolled her eyes. "And her time for settling that account came soon enough!"

Chapter 21

**

May 1936

From the kitchen Hattie heard Bobbi groan awake from a fourteen-hour sleep. It was just after 6pm, the east-facing living room was darkening quickly. A sudden clattering from the front room meant Bobbi had knocked things off the coffee table again.

Bobbi's weak voice floated into the kitchen.

"Hattie? Hattie?"

Hattie shouted back. "What?"

"I'm carrying a baby, Hattie. You hear?"

Hattie came to the doorway. "Another singer in this world? Ain't near big enough."

Bobbi dug through the spilled magazines and ashtray, and fished out her spoon and a bag of brown heroin.

"But this monkey is killin' me honey and I'm afraid it's gonna kill the child."

She bent the spoon and made flame with the lighter. In seconds the mixture bubbled. Hattie came in and sat down on the divan. "Do you want this child?"

"I don't think so." Bobbi drew the solution into a needle and tested it. "Did you want yours?"

Hattie re-tied the bandana on her hair. "No, I surely didn't."

Bobbie shook off a slipper and brought her foot up.

"Why'd you keep it then?"

Hattie turned to face Bobbi. "I just looked at the child in my heart and I say 'Oh honey, just cause your daddy took women don't mean you got to pay for his crimes with your life."

The singer shook her head. "Well I look at the child in my heart and say, I'm real sorry honey, but I got me a career."

Bobbi shot up between her toes. "Hattie, I'm touring with Ellington, I got me the hottest blues record in history, I outsell Bessie Smith." She groaned with the rush and laid her head back. "I'm Bobbi Savoy!"

Hattie raised her eyebrows. "So, you don't want the baby?"

"I'm a selfish, evil woman Hattie, I straight out admit it. I want to sing and get high then I want to die, ain't nothing in there about raisin' no baby."

Bobbi stumbled to the window and made some awkward dance moves. "You know I started my career dancing? Just a walk-on in a contest, that's all. But the orchestra leader thought he saw something special and asked me to sing."

She gazed out at 125th Street in the darkness.

"Hattie, the doctors are givin' me a few more years

unless I change my ways which I ain't gonna do. What business I got bringing in a baby to that world where she winds up like me?"

Hattie jumped up. "Nothin about you and her is the same. You was raped and abandoned. Raised by a trumpet and a piano. But that child is gonna have love all around, and if it's a girl, well, she won't be messed with I promise you that. And she'll learn to stay clear of the mistakes her mama made."

"How can you be sure of that?" Bobbi spun around. "You sayin' you'll be her second mama?"

Hattie was thinking. "Maybe the daddy wants the baby, you ask him yet?"

"No honey, he's a musician, wants nothing to do with this."

Bobbi stared in Hattie's large brown eyes. "You gonna be there, Hattie? Tell me now."

Hattie smiled. "Put it this way, baby. I'm gonna find me a good man and he and I gonna have a big family, and you and your child will fit right in." Hattie searched her friend's face. "Now, you gonna say who the daddy is?"

"Just some cat I met on the road, baby. Couple of months ago. No name."

Hattie frowned "Child needs a name. Basie? Ellington? Armstrong? You were in Los Angeles a couple of months ago." Hattie remembered the timing. "Sure enough that's where it happened." She smiled at Bobbi. "You was probably too drunk to remember!"

"Naw baby, I remember just fine. A San Francisco child. I bedded this one in the City by the Bay." Bobbi stroked the arm of her friend. "You got a problem with my love life, baby?"

Hattie fixed her gaze on the black void outside the window. "No more nameless babies." She turned to her friend. "I don't crave men, like you do, I guess."

Bobbi turned to her purse and sighed. "I don't crave nothing 'cept this damn heroin. But three months of travelin' is a long time for this girl to go without some male company. One man same as the next though, honey. Truly."

Bobbie took Hattie's hand and kissed it. "But you are so rare, so good to me. Oh, Hattie I'm so glad you came into my life, what would I do, what would I do . . .'"?

**

James Pierce slipped off his coat and rolled up his sleeves.

"Sounds like you got more than you bargained for in a roommate! What happened to Bobbi's pregnancy? Did she go to term?"

Hattie slipped a press photo of Bobbi out of the bag and examined it. "According to the doctors Bobbi had zero chance of havin' a healthy baby. Or even a live one."

**

September 1936

The spring rains were heavy. Hattie sat on the corner of the bed, cleaning sweat off a writhing Bobbi Savoy in the back bedroom on 125th Street. The singer was glassy-eyed, her bulging nightgown twisted and wet.

"Baby's gonna be a girl, Hattie assured her struggling friend. "I just know it. And listen, she's singing to you Bobbi, can't you hear? "Hmmmm. I'm gonna be here in the morning …" Hattie sang in a low voice. "You're all I got so take me home, yeah, I'm gonna be here in the morning, hmmm-hmmmm-mmmm."

In the kitchen a pot of boiling water sterilized towels.

Bobbi's breathing had become shallow and rapid. Hattie leaned over and shook her.

"Bobbi look at me, listen to me. There's a baby counting on you. Name of Lovae, remember? Lovae's coming, Bobbi, and you gotta be her mama. You can't die, cause you ain't allowed to take the child with you. And you can't have no dope right now."

There was no response. Hattie took her wrist and found no pulse. She grabbed the pitcher and threw the water in her friend's face.

"You get back here, girl!" she screamed.

Bobbi sputtered and moaned.

Hattie ran to the phone and dialed. There was still no answer at the Ellington's. The police and hospital had been called twice but hadn't responded yet.

Then water flushed out of Bobbi's body. Hattie propped up her knees and confirmed dilation. She ran to the kitchen and fished out a hot towel with a wooden spoon. Minutes became hours. Bobbi thrashed and moaned in drug withdrawal at the same time she pushed out the baby. The labor lasted ten hours. In the end the child was stillborn.

Bobbi was devastated, trembling and weak. She struggled to take the baby from Hattie but was pushed back to the bed.

"Stop it Bobbi, there's nothing you can do unless you want to pray with me, hear? Now, woman, now's the time to quit feelin' sorry for yourself and pray for this girl's soul the best you can!"

Hattie took the lifeless Lovae and washed her clean.

"I can't pray!" Bobbi sat on her knees, her face pale, her body shaking. "I'm a dope addict! I don't even want this baby!" Then the crooner fell over gagging and sobbing. "I want my medicine!"

Hattie marched through the room holding the infant in an oversized blanket. "Lord I am the worst sinner to draw breath and I know it. And this woman here, she ain't much better. But this child ain't done a thing wrong, this Lovae is innocent as your son Jesus, and Lord you can punish me and Bobbi all you want, but please bless the child. God bless the child."

Bobbi passed out on the bed and began snoring.

Hattie closed her eyes on welling tears, her voice moaning, "God bless the child. God bless the child." Finally exhausted, and holding the still child, Hattie collapsed in the wooden chair and began mouthing the words God bless the child until sleep came.

Bobbi's insistent voice penetrated Hattie's dream.

"Hattie honey, look at this."

Hattie blinked open and focused on Bobbi holding a small blanket-covered package to her breast. "Lovae is hungry, Hattie."

Hattie the mid-wife pulled the edge of the blanket away and witnessed the baby feeding voraciously.

"What happened, Bobbi?"

"Merry Christmas baby!" The new mother smiled as her tears fell on Lovae's cheek. She looked up. "It's like you kept sayin Hattie, 'God bless the child!' And look!"

**

Hattie smiled. "Well it wasn't too long Bobbi signed up with Benny Goodman and she planned a long tour, a few years. She turned the apartment over to me, and promised to pay half the rent as long as I helped Lovae. She had the money now, and hired a full-time nanny up near Central Park in a fine suite.

"I made arrangements to bring her home with me on weekends. Anyway, you see, Jamal and I, we hoped to get married when he came off the road and have our first baby. I knew his name would be Reuben if it were a boy. Reuben was my father's middle name. I had the notion Lovae and Reuben might become like brother and sister. Little did I know!"

"Little did you know... what?"

Chapter 22

**

November 1936

Hattie exited the bus at Lexington and high-stepped around the snow piles. Evening was descending on Harlem, and the club scene wasn't jumping yet.

Speed Garron passed by in his Model A and pulled over. He waved Hattie into the car and soon enough they were warming up in a booth at the Savoy Grille. Garron ordered coffee, Hattie tea.

Garron seemed edgy. "Hattie, you want to buy my car?"

Hattie was flabbergasted. "Why Speed Garron what am I Going to do with a car when I only got one place to go and the bus gets me there perfectly fine." She paused. "How in the world you gonna get around to the clubs and check out the new talent without your car?"

"I lost my job as a booking agent for the Cotton Club and Bobbi is starting a two-year tour with Benny Goodman." Garron stared into his coffee.

"Hattie, I lost both my meal tickets at the same time, and I'm almost broke. I got to do something."

"Don't blame Bobbi, honey. A woman got to make hay while the sun shines. We all do."

"I suppose . . ."

A shade of anger crept into his voice. "I just know I'm the wrong color for Harlem these days. I can't get an act booked anywhere. Tuxedo, Cotton, Connie's, Smalls . . ."

"Speed baby, now you can't take it personally, Harlem is in the middle of a Negro renaissance that's shakin' the whole world, can't blame the cats for dealing with their own. But you know there's a place for you, you too good at what you do."

"What do I do Hattie? I'm a pimp. A talent pimp."

"You a middle-man that knows what works, baby." Hattie frowned. "Your client Bobbi worked out too good. Girl's too big for Harlem anymore."

"A big junkie." Speed nodded his head slightly. "I wonder if we may be seein' her for the last time." He smacked his hand on the table, causing customers to look around. "She broke faith with me," he snapped. "Me! Her own agent. I booked her first gig, you know. I'm the one who fought to get her a steady club date at Smalls. I improved her deal at the Tuxedo. I covered for her a hundred times when she was wasted. Where's the gratitude? Where's the loyalty?"

"She's in her own world, baby."

"Yeah? Well she's in your world too Hattie, a lot more than you know."

Hattie peered into his eyes. "What you mean?"

Garron shifted, looking away. "I mean, who do you think is the real father of Lovae?"

"Some cat in San Fran…"

"Not today, honey." He checked for eavesdroppers. "Try your man Jamal Handler. Knocked her up in Pasadena, I saw the two of them together plenty."

Hattie sat frozen.

"Yeah that's right, Hattie. The drugged-out whore you live with, she seduced your man right under your nose. God knows how many times. I bet they planned it all around when you'd be gone at work."

Hattie stared at her tea for a long moment. "Jamal and I weren't together that way. We was still courting when he left for his own tour."

Garron waved his hand. "Well, he sure had that kind of relationship with your best friend Bobbi Savoy. How could she call you a friend and stab you in the back? That's my question."

**

Hattie's recollection to Pierce came with closed eyes.

"Well Mr. Pierce. Cold weather or not I walked the seven blocks back to the apartment. I just felt little by little the human trust I was raised with, was being eaten away by life."

"So, did you confront either of them?"

Her eyes flashed wide open at the question. "Oh yeah."

**

Christmas 1936

Hattie cleaned up the place from the usual Friday night blow-out. At two o'clock in the afternoon Bobbi came stumbling into the kitchen and collapsed at the table.

"Hey baby, pour me some of last night's mud and make it right, you know."

Hattie swished the cold coffee in the percolator and poured it into a cup. Then she added chocolate syrup and two shots of gin. Bobbi drained half the cup and wiped off her mouth.

"Whew!"

"So, Bobbi, when do you leave for tour?"

"Real soon, baby. A long one too, out of this cold weather." She lit a cigarette. "Things change, don't they? Good bye Ellington, hello Benny Goodman."

Hattie's voice changed. "You gonna keep Lovae where she is?"

"Of course. That's a good place for her, and as long as I can afford it she'll get the best."

"You get any help from the father?" Hattie pitched the rag into the sink.

Bobbi turned. "I don't need help, baby. What you asking?"

Hattie glowered at the seated Bobbi. "I'm askin' if Lovae's father plans to marry you or is gonna help raise the girl. That's all I'm asking, Bobbi."

"Oh I get it." The singer waved off the implication. "Baby, you know there's lots of closeness with all these musicians and there's booze and drugs and you know damn well what's gonna happen."

"Bobbi, you told me this baby got made in San Francisco by some man you said was same as all the others. You was lying honey, that man is my man, Jamal Handler, and we were gonna marry and I was supposed to be the woman carryin' his child. Not you."

"Oh, I see that ofay Garron been talking to you." Bobbi stood up and turned her narrow sloe-eyes on Hattie.

"You got any idea where you are, pretty girl? You in New York City. You come up here from some slave town and think you gonna moralize to me about marriage and family?"

Hattie was near the boiling point. "I don't sing or dance or hobnob with the fancy elites out there Bobbi. I don't party all day and all night, and I don't have ten men at my door. Audiences don't worship me, and millions of people don't buy my records. I throw a mop. It's all I'll ever do. I'm just looking for one man and some kids. Simple as that."

Bobbi laughed. "You on the wrong street for that. Those damn seeds get into whoever they get into, honey, I don't keep a diary. Besides what you care about who that man been with anyway, long as he's there for you. You jealous of me? Go do somethin with your own good looks."

Hattie held back the tears. "All in the world I want is a baby with a name. Just because you ain't got a lick of motherhood in you, don't mean you can destroy my future as a mother to my own child. But that's what you're doin', takin' my man away before we get that chance."

Bobbi turned to walk out. "Honey, you go preach to somebody else cause I've got to get my medicine and get out of here before I throw you back where you came from."

**

Pierce grimaced. "That must have hurt."

"Well there comes a time when life is more than grooving on the music, comes a time for accountability." Hattie shook her finger. "She should have been honest with me. She knew Jamal was planning on being with me."

"Any repercussions?"

Hattie looked up. "I didn't see Lovae for the next ten years."

Chapter 23

Pierce returned from the rest room.

"Tell me about your guardian angel, your silent advocate."

Hattie stared out the window, then shook her head. "We don't need to dwell too much on him."

"Fine." Pierce checked his watch. A half hour remained on the ninety minutes. "Your interview."

"Then in 1938 there was a new newspaper in town." Hattie sat forward, grinning. "The New York Daily Record! I bought the first copy, you know. The Personal Advice column jumped out at me and became a real good lamp unto these big old feet. That kind of practical wisdom was exactly what I needed. You've changed the writer a few times in sixty-seven years but the truth always gets said, and I still read it every day."

"That's nice to hear." Pierce lifted his eyes. "Something changed in your love life. According to your notes and the rap sheet you had a baby in 1939."

"Ain't that something?" Hattie grinned. "Jamal Handler came back from his West Coast life and looked me up. He asked me to reconsider, said he never lied to me, he just never admitted things that weren't my business. Well somehow, he knew everything about my past few years, and that was all right because he'd been through the same thing and recovered."

"You got married?" He read some more. "Or not?"

"We never did get married but had a boy, and sure enough called him Reuben. Well there were complications and I couldn't have any more children. So, Reuben was it."

"You settled down somewhere?"

"More or less. Jamal lost his band when he moved back, so he took a gig with Art Blakely and the Jazz Messengers playing mostly New York clubs. Then in 1942 the war started and Jamal was drafted into an all-black Naval unit. His ship was sunk and then it was just Reuben and me."

"Wait." Pierce wrinkled his large forehead. "Jamal Handler was killed in World War Two?"

"February 1945. Iwo Jima G4 support ship." She cocked her head. "What you thinking, Mr. Pierce?"

Pierce stared at her, his hands on his hips. "So Reuben went to work with you every day?"

"Papoose style. Oh, that worked out just fine, and he became the mascot of so many of the Times people, you know. At four years old he knew their names, and their jobs. Knew every department of that newspaper, and the people who ran them. In 1945 he started going to school but it was clear from the beginning this boy was cut out to work for the New York Times as a journalist. But there wasn't going to be any future or him without an advanced education, that I knew right well. The more the better."

"Admirable." Pierce pursed his lips. "How were planning to finance that?"

"I could put just a few dollars away for his higher education each week, but I quickly saw that wasn't gonna do it, not for the better colleges anyway."

"Not too many scholarships in those years, either." Pierce raised his eyebrows. "Sounds like you needed a benefactor, yes?"

Hattie looked away. "Well looks like I'm gonna tell you about my friend, after all."

"Suit yourself."

**

Summer 1948

I just set this old mop down and walked on over to the windows with this notebook and find myself thinking about Reuben. I could write a thousand essays on this boy. It doesn't matter if he's white or black, those clear eyes, that easy smile and contagious enthusiasm would win the hardest hearts, even if he were striped like a zebra. But he's in eighth grade this year. In five years, I'll need a lot of money for his education. Saving more than a few dollars a month is difficult in this job. I'm thinking about the options, including the one I received this morning.

The Maintenance manager stopped Hattie as she walked through the service door.

"Hattie, there's a note left for you with the guard. Be quick about reading it. And don't be taking your mail here."

"Yes sir, I sure won't."

She opened the fancy linen envelope with the floral border. The note was hand-written in calligraphy and difficult to decipher. But she quickly enough understood. With trepidation Hattie took the service elevator to the fifth floor.

Reporters and secretaries arriving at work stopped to stare at the charwoman wandering through the New York Times hallways without a mop. She found the name and knocked on the obscured-glass door, her heart in her throat.

A smiling man in a bowtie and suit opened the door and invited her in.

"Miss Plain! Thank you for seeing me, I promise not to keep you. Do you by any chance remember me?"

"You're Benson Ridges, the Features writer. Dining, theatre and gardening. You made it possible for me to return to my job almost ten years ago after I recovered from my, uh, illness. I'm much obliged."

"Yes, I'm flattered you remember me. I have obviously known of you for some time. In fact, I have several essays you wrote and gave to Mr. Meyers years ago. I can't tell you how much I enjoyed reading them. Your freshness is truly exhilarating."

"Umm huh. What did you want to see me about, Mr. Ridges?"

"Miss Plain… may I call you Hattie?"

"Call me anything you want, Mr. Ridges."

"Hattie. There is something that . . . well, I have observed you nearly every day for . . . Hattie, I have an overwhelming desire to know you better. What I mean is, I have known you for over twenty years but you haven't had a chance to know me. Now I know there's difficulties inherent in what I'm proposing, but could you consider making time in your life for me? It's 1945 and people's attitudes are truly changing about . . . who can be with who."

Hattie turned to the window. This was beyond anything she could even imagine. She was 39 years old and not getting younger. He was white.

"Benson Ridges, I don't know what to say."

"Hattie. Look, my family has money. I can help you and Reuben. I can set up an education trust for him and use my family influence to get him into any school in the country. The three of us can live in the city, and you could write important things. I can help you get them published. Hattie will you think about what I'm asking . . . can we agree to talk again?"

Hattie's eyes widened. "You want to… marry me?"

Ridges drew closer and touched her shoulder. "I do. Hattie, I have loved you forever."

**

Pierce threw up his hands. "This is incredible."

Hattie stretched her legs. "No question he could give Reuben and me more than we ever thought possible. And he loved me! I believe that, I truly do."

"You didn't consider his offer?"

The old woman leaned on the desk and searched Pierce's face.

"Mr. Pierce, I don't know how to be a white woman." She sighed deeply. "And he had no idea the strains and pressures he'd be putting on himself, Reuben and me."

The boss nodded. "Things have certainly changed."

"Well I listened to this man of privilege confess his feelings for me and I was truly overcome. Problem was, I didn't love him. When he was done with his confession, he looked away, feeling a little stranded, I think. I held his hand. Then I kissed him on his forehead, and don't you know a tear fell from my eye and landed on his cheek. He reached up and touched it. Neither of us said a word." Hattie's voice trailed off. "I ran back to my job."

"Hmm. So that was the end of Benson, Bobbi and Lovae in your life? Big loss."

"Nothing is ever lost Mr. Pierce."

Chapter 24

**

November 1948

Hattie went to the front door despite the fact nobody gave up a name when she asked on the intercom. Standing in the mottled shade of the blooming Hickory stood a tall girl with pale brown skin framed by wavy black curls perfectly coiffed. Her tailored suit definitely came from Bergdorf's or Saks.

"Hello my name is Lovae Crowley." Green eyes added to her ethereal beauty. "I am looking for Miss Hattie Plain."

Hattie reached out and grabbed her. "Oh, Lovae you miracle. God bless the child!"

The two women went into the apartment, Hattie fixed tea and sandwiches.

"I need to know everything about you since I saw you last, baby, so start with the beginning. I lost track of your mother. She went on tour forever. When she came back, I'd lost contact, you know. With both of you."

Lovae was measured, slightly distant. Hattie attributed it to her influential uptown caregivers.

"Auntie Hattie, the last thing I remember was you standing at the window of the limousine, crying. The car took off and you ran into the apartment. I was three years old. I don't remember anything else that happened when I was three, but I recall that clearly."

"Aw honey, I was just 23 years old myself and your mother was a real big part of my life. So, when she became a big star and you went into boarding school, well I was a little bit stranded. I saw you on weekends for a while."

Hattie poured the tea.

"Mother stayed on tour for almost all my life, Auntie Hattie. I was raised up in Manhattan until last week when they told me I would have to leave."

"Leave?" Hattie examined her young friend's fearful eyes. "Now why would that ever come to pass?"

Lovae walked to the window and stared at the Hickory branches. "I don't know for sure, but I think mother stopped paying them."

"Excuse me honey. I got to make a phone call."

Hattie went to the hallway and dialed the tabletop phone.

A gruff voice answered. "What?'

"Speed?"

"Who is this?"

"Hattie Plain, Speed. Don't hang up on me. Just tell me one thing. What's happened to Bobbi?"

In a minute Hattie walked out to the living room.

"Lovae, your mother collapsed two weeks ago in Cleveland at the Statler Hotel. She was taken to a hospital and she's still there for now."

"Cleveland? That's only four or five hundred miles, we can get there by train in two days."

Hattie squeezed her hand. "There's more. She is canceling the rest of the tour. Lovae, she's broke. She won't be in that hospital past tonight."

"My mother broke? Auntie Hattie, I thought she was one of the most famous women in America. How can she be out of money?"

"Well now I think maybe she had a real expensive life style you know. Big staff of people following her around, eatin' out at the fine places."

"And the medicine."

"And the medicine."

Lovae tossed her head back. "Well that means she can't pay for me anymore. That's good though. I didn't like being in that place, and they didn't like me. All the money was wasted."

"No honey, you got a good education and you look real good too."

For the first time Hattie could see Jamal in her face. "Nothing's ever wasted."

Lovae clenched her fist and relaxed it, again and again, an action which did not go unnoticed by Hattie.

"What is it, baby. Your hand goes to sleep?"

"Auntie Hattie I have a disease and none of the doctors know what it is. It might be this, might be that. Anyway I'm having a hard time walking. And there's other things."

Hattie gazed through the window at the Hickory, which was blooming again. Birds had returned to its budding branches. She smiled and took Lovae's hand.

"Well baby, things go full circle, don't they? Maybe it's time to know your mama again."

**

James Pierce mumbled. "I had the feeling we were getting Bobbi Savoy back into the story."

Hattie stared at the ceiling. "I made a few calls and found Bobbi in a flophouse over on 3d. At least they had the decency to throw her back in my town. She was a mess, reminded me of how I must have looked at one time." Hattie shrugged. "She came to my place and spent two months getting clean. Lovae was a big part of her recovery."

For a moment Hattie seemed lost in the memory.

"I explained to Reuben what had happened and how we were gonna step in and help this lady that had helped me so much at one time. He was getting on to fourteen years old and I knew he'd understand. And he did."

"So, did Bobbi recover?"

"Bobbi got her groove back a little. Singin' a little here and there. Then when she was feeling strong, I contacted Speed Garron and he booked her into the Tuxedo. Bobbi's first comeback appearance was a little shaky but then she sold out the Tuxedo for two solid years."

Pierce shrugged. "Sounds like things were restored."

Hattie waved her hand.

"At the end of two months she and Lovae found their own place in the East Village. Bobbi bought a Cadillac automobile and oh my how those two got to know each other. But Lovae had adopted me, and I think Bobbi was a little jealous."

"So you got Bobbi back from the dead. Was she clean?"

"No, she used. But less than ever. I really felt she was making the effort."

"So happily ever after?" He studied the rap sheet. "Or not?"

"Well Speed Garron was staying busy with more than booking club dates. He now had an uptown brothel of very expensive girls."

"Ah . . ."

"That made me think long and hard about where Reuben's college money was gonna come from. More than once I picked up the phone to ask Benson Ridges for a date, but each time I hung up. You see, taking advantage of honest people is the worst thing I can think of."

Pierce arched an eyebrow. "Even if they volunteer for it?"

Hattie narrowed her eyes. "*Especially* if they volunteer for it, Mr. Pierce."

"Let's go back to the problem of finding money for Reuben's college."

"I thought it through pretty good. If I had to give myself up for financial gain, I'd just as soon rent myself out, not sell myself. Couldn't tell him that though."

"You mean . . ."

"I met with Speed a few times, we talked about Bobbi's amazing career comeback, of course. But I was interested in hearing all about the way his girls made their money."

"Did you find out what you needed to know?"

"Hmm, is the day long? I was ready in a month. I never told Speed that was what I planned to do, cause you know that's a competitive trade. Organized crime had been moving in since prohibition ended fifteen years earlier. No, you had to be real careful, as Speed later found out."

"What do you mean?"

"He got too big, flashed his money around. Cadillacs. Girls on his arm. Stork Club, Tavern on the Green, Park Avenue Hotel, I mean to say this boy was living high. Well you know they found his body in the East River floating in several barrels. Out of business, but it was predictable."

Pierce paced the room, pausing in front of her.

"Ms. Plain." They stared at one another for a long moment. "You have a certain detachment from death that I've never seen before."

Hattie rolled her eyes. "That what's botherin' you, Mr. Pierce? Would you prefer I leave a little piece of myself behind every time this world takes another friend or family member? I wouldn't weigh too much now would I?"

"There's got to be times when it all catches up . . ."

"First of all, Mr. Pierce, I don't believe death is anything but a door that we all gonna go through. And second, you must not have been listening when we talked about it catchin' up with me and my going crazy and getting committed to the asylum. Were you listenin' Mr. Pierce? Or was that cruel statement just the reporter in you looking for a reaction?"

Pierce held up a hand. "You're right, it's about my propensity to dig out the ironies in a story, and I apologize."

"That's fine. I'm just checkin' on you." Hattie smiled.

"Now you may wonder what's this pretty thirty-something janitor gonna do to make sure her boy gets the right education?"

Pierce shrugged. "I'm afraid to ask."

Hattie sighed. "I still had a number of contacts from back in the day. So, I set up a call service for the elite of Manhattan and Harlem. Borrowed five hundred dollars from Bobbi and bought nice clothes." She wagged her ancient head with a sad smile. "Mr. Pierce, I was ready."

Chapter 25

"Ready? For what?" Pierce fumed. "There's no way you were prepared for that kind of life, Miss Plain. Prostitution is the dark side of this city. Back then, women in that line of work were routinely savaged or killed. Still are. And face it, you weren't... experienced."

"Well, Mr. Pierce, you know these men were pretty much decent characters, just looking for some strange mostly. Black and white, good and evil. I wasn't prudish, I did what they wanted done. I serviced them good."

Hattie shook her head. "Mr. Pierce, you got to strive to be best at anything you do." Brightening up, she added, "And I charged for it, honey. Put that money away for Reuben's education, every dime. Paid Bobbi her five hundred in two months. The money I needed for Reuben wasn't gonna come in overnight. It would take a few years. But you know Mr. Pierce, I had nothing but years to give."

**

February 1953

> *Got arrested again last night. I don't know how much longer I can entertain men for money. They know me as Lady M, the*

Harlem mystery girl, the infamous connection to musicians and entertainers, writers and gangsters. Dangerous Lady M who can throw them down and laugh, pour drinks over their faces and give them a time they'll never get from any decent woman. Little do they know I haven't seen a writer, musician or gangster in fifteen years! I'm just Hattie, and I throw a mop! Truth is, I hate appealing to the dark side of men just to enrich myself. It sure isn't right for either of us. I lose respect, just like they're trying to do. I always feel guilty going to church, cause I hate hypocrites too. Well maybe two more years, Reuben will be seventeen then, and ready for college. And the money will be there, all fifteen thousand dollars, maybe more.

I often think about the man who really wanted me, the exquisitely sad Benson Ridges. My hope is he never finds out what I do for money. But it's best this way, I'll quit when I have enough for Reuben, then it's all about him and how far he can take it. Meanwhile I have to handle this bail and court fine. Occupational hazard, the lawyer calls it. Just the cost of doing business.

**

Pierce shot a rubber band against a picture on the wall.

"I'm confused. Almost twenty years earlier you swore to the memory of your parents and Ponce Davis that you were going to honor their sacrifices and do the right thing the rest of your life. Did I get that wrong?"

"Right and wrong ain't the same for everybody all the time. Depends."

"Really! On what?"

"On the motive, Mr. Pierce."

"Oh? So, you do what you have to do to serve a higher purpose?" He made a face. "Isn't that an argument the Klan would have used?"

"The Klan used violence to keep people down. Reuben needed an education to break that cycle. And me, well I had certain temporary assets that could make that happen. Mr. Pierce, where's the greater sin, taking money for sex work with strangers or marrying a self-loathing white man, and hoping that Reuben doesn't get too confused by it?"

Pierce winced. "You're lucky you didn't get a disease."

"Ha!" Hattie shrugged. "Caught a bad infection once or twice, and had to take medication for a while. I took too much, too long I think, cause they busted me on that too." Hattie snickered. "Lord Almighty, I never got away with nothing!"

"Except killing those Tennessee hoodlums."

Hattie tapped her fingers on the armchair.

"Just keeping the conversation honest." Pierce rubbed his face. "Well apparently your supplemental night work didn't interfere with the rest of your life."

"I never gave up the baseline job, if that's what you mean. Working the mop for the *Times*." She broke a wry smile. "You never know when the cash cow gonna dry up."

"But you got it done." Pierce nodded. "Reuben turned out, did he not?"

The old woman let out a laugh. "Oh my yes! He was straight A's in high school. Interned at the Times in the afternoons, not easy for a black man in the nineteen-fifties. Reuben picked City College of New York and went through it with a perfect 4 point 0. He was accepted into Columbia School of Journalism for his master's degree. Graduated in 1962. My son took a year to intern in Washington DC. He got caught up in the Kennedy Administration and became an assistant to White House Press Secretary Pierre Salinger!"

James was curious. "But he came back to New York?"

Hattie closed her eyes and relished the picture. "Reuben came back in late 1963, shook-up by the assassination. The Times had a job ready for him; assignment— the brand new Civil Rights desk. That had a very good future."

Pierce smiled. "So he took the *New York Times* by storm!"

"Almost." Hattie took a deep breath. "Christmas day, one week from starting his new job with the Times, the police shot and killed Reuben on his way home from a restaurant. Trudy's Ribs parking lot. Mistaken identity. There had been a robbery nearby. Wrong man, wrong place."

Pierce went silent for a long time. "I am sorry."

Hattie remained upbeat. "But I've learned that every moment has to stand on its own, Mr. Pierce. Like an angel, it comes out of nowhere, burns bright for whatever time, then it's a memory. Served its purpose though. The investment in Reuben won't be wasted."

Pierce looked away. "Good."

Hattie spoke quietly. "Reuben lives, you know."

Chapter 26

December 1963

Bobbi Savoy's lean frame was draped in a royal blue dress, perched regally in a designer divan wheeled onstage to a packed Club Tuxedo. Enthusiasm turned into standing applause as the house lights came up.

"Still lookin' good, Bobbi," boomed an admirer.

She murmured her thanks. The stage went dark except for a single spotlight. The aging singer addressed the room with a damaged voice and watery eyes.

"This is for you, Hattie. And you, Lovae. And you too, Edith Plummer Crowley."

She smiled faintly at her own self-depreciating humor. A horn blew soft notes as she began "God Bless the Child." Hattie took a sharp breath and closed her eyes. Lovae reached over and squeezed her hand. The room went silent as the legendary crooner brought up the words, low and throaty. No one cared that her voice was uneven. Bobbi held the room through the last chorus, which was half sung, half spoken.

Mama may have, Papa may have
But God bless the child that's got his own
That's got his own
He just worry about nothin'
Cause he's got his own
©Billie Holiday / Arthur Herzog Jr.

The last note disappeared, and Bobbi bowed her head. As the light faded, Hattie and Lovae both saw the microphone slip from her hand onto the cushion. A moment went by. Then came the deafening response.

A Klieg light swung out to catch Hattie's reaction as the divan retracted offstage. From her booth Hattie smiled, waved, and blew a kiss with one hand. With the other she stroked Lovae's hair who had now collapsed in Hattie's lap, her uncontrolled sobbing unnoticed in the thundering applause.

**

Hattie was lost in thought as Pierce paced the office.

"Bobbi Savoy died in 64, right? Complications they said, always complications." He stopped at the window. "It was flat-out drugs, wasn't it?"

"She died that night." Hattie shook her head. "You know Mr. Pierce, I couldn't tell you if it was the drugs or the hepatitis or the cancer, the bad liver, bad kidneys or bad heart. This poor woman was a walking medical journal, but most of her troubles came from her life style. She knew it was comin' and didn't help herself one bit, believe me."

Hattie adjusted herself in the chair. "But as they say, 'There but for the grace of God . . .' "

Pierce scowled. "Don't say that."

"Don't say what?"

"'There but for the grace of God.'" He sat forward and smacked his hand on the chair. "You had every opportunity to go down the same path but you said no. You made a better choice."

Hattie thought for a minute. "I chose a crooked path myself sometimes too. We can't sit in judgment of her."

"Why not?" Pierce stood. "She made very public choices. She seduced us, then rammed our faces in it."

"She wanted to die, Mr. Pierce." Hattie looked up. "How do you judge that?"

April 1981
Miss Hattie Plain Honorary Mayor, 125th Street
Harlem New York

Dear Ms. Plain

I am Ralph Benjamin Waters, publisher of the East Hattiesburg Caller, a newspaper published primarily for the local African-American voice here in southern Mississippi. I am in receipt of your letter written almost two years ago. It was given to me by Mitchell Tomlinson of the Hattiesburg Chamber of Commerce and is on my desk as I write.

You should know the East Hattiesburg Caller has been in and out of business several times since your unfortunate departure. After the fire and untimely assassination of Mr. Ponce Davis, the paper was re-started in 1930 by two gentlemen from New Orleans. The depression put them out of business in 1932. Another investor started up operations in 1937, also naming it the East Hattiesburg Caller. He sold it in 1956 to a chain of black newspapers. They closed it in 1974, the year the floods took out the entire black commercial and residential district around Mobile Street. By the way the area never recovered, and the residents relocated with government assistance.

My father bought the rights and the masthead in 1978 and we commenced publication of a weekly newspaper in 1979 reaching out to people of color now broadly dispersed. My father passed shortly after the first issue, and I have been handling the duties of Managing Editor since that time.

As regards J.J. Ketchum, there's no obituary published over the last twenty years anywhere in the tri-county area, we checked exhaustively. My brother-in-law Mitchell is a fraternity brother to Sheriff Lamar "Beau" Gurning. They may have talked about your charges against the MIA Ketchum, I can't say.

> *Miss Plain consider yourself Editor Emeritus of the Caller. There is a space for you here, always. Your name is on our walls; your story had been printed in our paper. There are Hattie Plain for President buttons sold at local fairs and they always sell out!*
>
> *I send you the profound respect and love of this newspaper and pray daily to know Mr. Davis is happily producing the Heavenly Caller.*

> *Sincerely*
> *R.B. Waters, Publisher*

"So, this is in response to a letter you wrote in 1979 wherein you accused J.J. Ketchum of murder and arson?" Pierce laid the letter down. "Why would you decide to accuse those men so many years later?"

Hattie shook off her Nikes and sat back. "Read in the New York Times that the 1974 floods that destroyed East Hattiesburg had unearthed the remains of many souls buried in the fields. It took a few years for Federal forensic investigators to discover the truth."

Pierce turned. "Truth?"

March 1974

State geology engineers and a spokesman for Southern Mississippi University in Hattiesburg confirmed today the discovery of the skeletal remains of more than a dozen people unearthed by the centennial flooding,

which wiped out the southeast side of the city. According to sources close to the University, the bones bore characteristics of a hasty field burial.

February 1979

Mississippi chief pathologist Dr. Herman Miller told reporters today in a scheduled news conference that ten of the skeletons found washed out of a field near Hattiesburg, were probably victims of hanging, evidenced by separation of the neck vertebrae. Dr. Miller said no forensic evidence has been found which might help police identify the date or identity of the victims.

"So you think these deaths were the work of J.J. Ketchum?" "I ain't sayin that, Mr. Pierce. But it made the point to me that Klan elders were aging, and I was afraid they was gonna sneak through death's door without accountability to justice here. And that included Ketchum."

"Ah yes. Your 'inevitability of justice' theory." He knitted his hands behind his head and stared at the ceiling. "Time for you to finally face the devil, was it?"

"Or his offspring."

"You weren't looking forward to it?" Pierce joked.

Hattie joined him in the laugh, but then quickly went quiet.

"My man Job said, 'The thing I fear the most has come upon me.'" She adjusted her glasses. "Brother, I knew that feeling."

Chapter 27

**

July 1981

The charter bus rumbled down the Palmers Crossing off ramp, passing the sign, "Hattiesburg Mississippi, pop. 37,500". Hattie requested a stop. She managed to get herself and the overnight bag down the metal stairwell and onto the sidewalk as the bus roared away in a dusty cloud.

She looked up and down the intersection, recognizing nothing. There was fast food, a café built into a strip mall and a gas station. What part of Palmers Crossing was this? How far away was she from the site of her parents massacre? How far from Mr. Davis's last brave act . . . and the freedom riders terrified last stand? Why were her hands trembling?

The 67-year-old New Yorker took a deep breath and headed toward the gas station, already popping beads of sweat from the rising morning temperature and southern humidity.

Inside a bony attendant with stringy hair, soiled cap, handlebar moustache, and a red t-shirt watched her approach from his lounge chair.

Hattie walked right up to the counter.

"Is this the town of Palmers Crossing, sir?"

"Nope."

"But the sign says it is."

"Palmers Crossing road. The town's been gone a long time, part of Hattiesburg now." He smirked and reached for a fresh pack of cigarettes under the glass counter. "Lucky Hattiesburg, huh?"

"Where is it from here?"

He held his hand like a pistol and fired at the window. "Three miles." Hattie couldn't take her eyes off the dragon tattooed the length of his arm. A Grand Dragon maybe?

"Can you tell me where's a motel around here?"

He pointed at the highway. "Best you go on down to old town Palmers Crossing for that. That's where you'll find your nigra hotels and such."

A trucker came into the station and stepped in front of Hattie.

"Howdy, Bullet. That's fifty dollars on pump two. Bill the lumber company." Bullet opened a log and made an entry. The customer left.

"I guess he must not have seen me standing here." She looked around. "You got a restroom?"

"Yep." He nodded toward the keys hanging on the cash register. "Won't do you no good though."

Hattie folded her arms. "Why not?"

He smacked the new pack against his palm and tore it open.

"Out of order."

She looked around. "Well then I'll use the mens'."

The attendant smiled and lit up, puffing out a donut shaped ring. "It's out of order too."

Hattie's heart began pounding. Confrontation had already begun. "You sayin' I can't use the rest rooms?"

"You can use'm." He pushed himself out of the chair. "Just can't flush'm."

"What do you do all day sir, hold it in?"

"I pee behind the station. Wanna watch? Fifty cents, cash." His grinned revealed ruined teeth. "Café's right across the street." He pulled hard on the cigarette, held it for a moment, then blew smoke at her. "Mama."

Hattie turned to the door but stopped when she eyed a newspaper displayed in the steel rack. The East Hattiesburg Caller masthead grabbed her attention. She dropped a quarter and the rack opened. She removed a paper and closed it. It worked perfectly, the first small victory in Hattiesburg.

She walked across the street to the café and grille, used the ladies room and wound up sitting at a table near the counter.

The paper was thin, but she already felt the thrill of discovery. A waitress appeared.

"What will it be today, ma'am?"

Hattie looked up. "Scrambled eggs with wheat toast. You got grits today?"

"Honey, I got grits every day."

She held up the newspaper. "You know where this is printed in town?"

"No ma'am, I surely don't."

"You got a store named Ketchum's?"

"Honey, I'll put this order in and bring you a Yellow Pages. We got thirty-eight thousand people in Hattiesburg, two colleges and an Army camp."

"Camp Shelby?"

"Yes ma'am, my husband's in the reserves, works out there as a carpenter."

"My father worked in a mill . . ." Hattie allowed her memory to wander. The exchange across the street at the gas station left her nerves jangled. She mumbled quietly to herself. "Can't see him hanging from a rope can I, baby? I got to remember that strong man who stood up for me and faced down hatred with dignity."

The waitress bent over. "I'm sorry hon, were you sayin something?"

Hattie took a deep breath. "I'm just thinking back, it's all good."

"You visitin', hon?" The strawberry blonde smiled. "Comin back from somewhere maybe?"

Hattie relaxed. "How'd you know that?"

"This is a friendly town, hon. Don't know how it was before. I'll bring you the book."

In a few moments Hattie had the phone book at her table. She donned her glasses and began leafing through it. She was still studying it when breakfast came.

"You find what you're looking for, hon?"

"No." Hattie closed the book and moved it aside. "I'll dig it up though. Where's the closest motel?"

She stepped back and pointed. "Two blocks that way, hon. I'm Angie by the way. What's your name?"

The question surprised her. "Hattie Plain."

"Alright, Hattie Plain." The waitress signaled with her arm and moments later a toothless white man wearing a cook's cap and a red scarf appeared at her table.

"Hattie, this is PK Letterer, our cook. Tell him, he may know what you're looking for."

Letterer stood by quietly. Hattie wasn't sure he could hear anything. "I'm looking for a place that used to be called Ketchum's Dry Goods. You ever hear of that?"

The cook leaned forward and opened Hattie's newspaper. He took a pen and drew a circle around an ad, then went back to the kitchen.

"He don't say much, hon, but he cooks up a storm! I hope he was helpful."

"He said a lot, baby." Hattie folded the paper. "By the way, my first meal in Mississippi in fifty-one years was just fine. Thank you."

Hattie left a five-dollar tip and walked two blocks to the Budget Traveler motel.

It was almost eleven a.m. when she checked in. The clerk was a petite brunette about twenty years old dressed in a tan company vest.

"Good morning, and welcome. I'm Julie, how can I help you?"

Hattie set her bag down. "I need a room for a day or two. Julie."

"Perfect. Please fill out our little check-in form and we'll get you in a room right away. Will that be on a credit card?"

"Credit card?" Hattie shook her head. "I brought cash. Or else I got my checkbook with me."

"Hmm." The clerk pointed to the credit card policy in the wall. "Well, with proper ID we can take an out-of-state check. I'll need a Drivers License and a check guarantee card."

"Sister, I don't drive. And I never heard of a check Guarantee card. I got my bus pass and my New York Times ID, and Social Security card. That's what I got."

"I see. Well then, the deposit will be two hundred dollars for two days."

"Honey, I ain't got two hundred dollars. I got a round trip bus ticket and walkin'-around money."

Julie shook her head slowly. "Gosh I'm sorry."

"Sorry? Look here, I just came 1300 miles by bus, and I got cash to pay for a room and you telling me you're sorry?"

"I can take a cashier's check," chirped the clerk. "Or money order."

"Sounds like some economic Jim Crow goin' on."

A middle-aged black man turned around. His glasses sat low on his skinny nose, giving him an air of a disapproving school teacher. His hair was so short he appeared bald. His lavender shirt was double starched, his tie a perfect four-in-hand blue and red stripe. Dark blue suspenders hugged a trim physique. He drew Hattie aside.

"I'm Kenneth Robertson Goins, General Manager." Goins narrowed his eyes. "I'll give you some free advice, my sister. You in a free country to say whatever's on your mind. But don't you come around where I'm working and talk about Jim Crow. Uh-huh. You see, I worked with people who came to Hattiesburg on a bus to get rid of Jim Crow and gave their lives doing it. Some of them haven't been found to this day. But I'll tell you something about their sacrifice. Jim Crow is dead where I work. You hearing me?"

Hattie studied this man. She tried to imagine him seventeen years earlier meeting the boys as they got off the New York bus.

"Well bless your heart sir. I persuaded some of them young ones into coming down here on Freedom busses. Reverend Padgett used me because I was born and raised here."

"You knew Padgett?"

"I left this town over fifty years ago with my house on fire and my parents slaughtered and the Klan looking for me." She smiled. "Now I come back and I can't get a room from a brother cause I don't have a credit card? You mind telling me what happened?"

Goins smiled, and reached out for her hand. "Why, you're Hattie Plain, aren't you?"

Hattie nodded, surprised.

Eyes flooding, Goins clasped her hands in his. "Miss Plain, there's something called managers' discretion. Now, you fill out that application and I'll handle things. You're in the Grand Suite; Julie will carry your bag. Stay as long as you like. It's all on me. You need a ride, Clarence is at your service."

Hattie showered and napped. By three o'clock she was ready. She preferred riding the bus to old town, Hub City they used to call it. She exited at Forrest Street. Hattie recognized the layout. In the early days streetcars ran like spokes from the Hub to the outlying homes. The City Hall was a different color but just as imposing as it was in 1923 when it was built, and in 1929 when she tore past it, running for her life. The bronze sign proclaimed it an Historical Landmark.

Businesses and civic buildings ran for two blocks in every direction. She measured the scene from her memory. Ponce Davis's old printing plant would have been in the black district on the corner of Mobile Street, just about where the Hattiesburg Flood Control station now stood.

She remembered the wooden structure that exploded when the torches hit and in moments found herself hyperventilating. She began singing and walking until calm returned.

In less than a minute she located the address circled in the newspaper. She looked up. Painted on the high fascia were the faded words Ketchum Hardware and Dry Goods, but the doors and windows were modern, and advertised *Bigalow's Hardware* in gold leaf. Other signs indicated the place was part of a national chain. Drawing herself up, she entered the store.

**

The managing editor wagged his head. "So, let me get this straight. You found Ketchum's Dry Goods and walked right in?"

"I had to, James Pierce!"

"Oh, I know you had to, but I'm surprised you did it without an armed escort." He wagged his head and shuddered. "You a gutsy chick, Hattie Plain."

"I had two possible outcomes, Mr. Pierce. Either they would finally kill me, in which case I'd be with my family again. Or they wouldn't, in which case I planned to nail their asses."

Chapter 28

Hattie stood in this alien store, and knew it was too late to turn back. A teenage boy approached.

"Can I help you ma'am?"

Hattie scanned the store for an adult. "I'm looking for the owner, son."

"That would be my father James Bigalow. He's probably in the back office. May I inquire who's asking?"

"Are you related to the Ketchum family who started this store?"

"Yes ma'am, I'm Randall Bigalow. Mr. Ketchum is my great-grandfather. His father founded the store in 1884, same year as this town got started."

Hattie smiled at him. "Well I have roots here that go back over a hundred years myself and I would like to speak with your father please, young man."

He motioned to follow, and Hattie maneuvered the isles before reaching the rear of the store where she passed through a set of swinging doors. Several small built-out offices included a bathroom. It all led to the large warehouse area.

The youth spoke in low tones to a man inside the office. He stepped into the doorway.

"James Bigalow here ma'am, can I help you?"

Hattie turned and looked him over. "Mr. Bigalow, I am Hattie Plain. Does that name ring a bell with you?"

"No ma'am. Should it?"

"My father was Rupert Jones."

"Sorry. That name means nothing to me either."

"How about Miriam Jones?"

He paused. "Yes ma'am, we know something about her. She was the lone survivor of a family massacre years ago here in town."

"Is Mr. J.J. Ketchum still living?"

There was awkward silence. Bigalow was suspicious.

"I don't know who you are or what you want but I expect we're all done talking."

Hattie steadied herself. "Mr. Bigalow, I am that survivor."

He looked at Hattie with concern. "You're Miriam Jones…"

She took a deep breath. "Now I'm Hattie Plain." Her voice trembled, and she fought to stay conscious. "When it happened I was just a teenage girl . . ."

Hattie felt herself passing out and tried to grab the door. Bigalow threw his arms around her and helped her to the padded office chair.

"Are you all right? Sit here Miss Plain." He signaled to his son. "Water's on the way."

Hattie recovered quickly. For the next fifteen minutes she explained her childhood in Hattiesburg, her three years of part-time work with the Caller. She described the attack of the Klan, the killing of her aunt in the park by the Ketchum wagon. And she was able to describe her father's defense of the family. Then with great self-control Hattie told of the lynching of Davis, and the torching of the newspaper. Then she managed to describe what happened later that night which closed out her life in Hattiesburg.

"There's a lot of evil tradition right here, Miss Plain. I'll Be honest about it. My grandfather is an intolerable bigot."

Bigalow stood up. "But he was and is a great man in so many other ways. He and his father built and rebuilt this whole building and the business too, by hand, one plank at a time. He employed Indians and blacks and he paid them good wages. He sold to everybody, not just whites, and drew criticism for it. He was boycotted by white groups for handling Negro mercantile."

Hattie realized Mr. Bigalow was clearly practiced at this explanation.

"He offered credit to the poor; many ex-slaves owed him thousands of dollars, and never paid. He donated much of the construction money to the Mobile District high school."

Hattie flashed on the banker and the blueprints outside Mr. Davis's window. Who knew the financing came from J.J. Ketchum, three years before the local holocaust.

Hattie shook her head. "What took him down the path of terror?"

"I don't know. Fear I suppose. Peer pressure. Dismay at seeing the so-called serving class get 'uppity'." He looked down at the floor. "Increase in crime, angry out-of-control youth. Gangs. Fear of rape. Locked doors, guns at the ready."

Hattie listened. "Which side you talkin' about now?"

Bigalow nodded. "Fair enough. But have you ever been so fearful you find yourself able to justify any means?"

The picture of four half-naked men by the riverside came into her head. "Maybe . . ."

"Miss Plain I know this is going to be hard for you to bear, but I have something in the storage room worth seeing."

The trio traipsed across the cement warehouse to a corner. Bigalow pulled the cover off a steel-wheeled wagon with the faded name J.J. Ketchum painted on the side. He lowered his tone.

"I'm afraid this is probably the very instrument of your aunt's death, Miss Plain. Right here. We were going to restore this and put this on display at the new Hattiesburg museum. But now..."

Hattie looked over the wagon and touched his arm. "You go forward with that, Mr. Bigalow. Do, hear? With no mention of what happened. You see, life isn't about just one thing, life is about everything."

Images of her father standing in the wagon bed with a rope around his neck flashed in her mind. She inspected the warped planks of the old vehicle. There against the inside wall of the tailgate were two dark swipes visible through the dust.

"You see these marks?" Hattie almost choked out the words.

"Yes?"

"My daddy's heel made them as the wagon jerked forward." She recovered her poise. "You're wonderin' how I know? They're made of black oil, ox blood and glycerin. Homemade polish. Wore those shoes only to church. And to the after-church speech about Bessie Coleman in the little park. He went to jail that day, and still had them on them the next day when he was hanged in his yard. My yard."

Bigalow and his son remained respectfully quiet.

Hattie touched the sturdy but weather-corrupted vehicle.

"When you restore it, please save the heel marks. That's history right there."

"Miss Plain, may I be your sightseeing guide today? I'm sure there's much you want to revisit. And maybe some people too."

"To be perfectly honest with you, the last thing I expected was that the family of J.J. Ketchum would be my tour guide in this visit. Yes sir, I surely will take you up on that."

The Lincoln Town car crossed the city of Hattiesburg. Hattie Plain stared out the window. At her request they stopped at the park where the attack had taken place.

The zone of terror was now a baseball diamond. A stone memorial commemorated the event with a bronze plaque depicting a bird rising to flight.

Hattie almost ran to the spot where Bessie Coleman's sister spoke that fateful afternoon and waved toward the tree line.

"They came from over there!" she yelled.

"Yes, we know that." Bigalow nodded. "They run tours all the time, Miss Plain."

"The people tried to run… this is where she fell… my aunt." She touched third base where the woman was struck down by the wagon. "I like it better like this!" she laughed, looking over the groomed baseball diamond.

Jim Bigalow drove to the Palmers Crossing sign, then headed out to Hattie's birth home. As they made the final turn Hattie recognized the Hickory Tree. The car rolled to a stop.

Everything was different since the fire. A small store now stood where the house had been. The access road taken by the killer riders and their death wagon that fiery night was now a parking lot for the nearby golf course. But the Witness Tree, the Hickory planted on the Jones property line continued to bear silent testimony to the grisly history.

Hattie approached the ancient tree, imagining her modest home behind it. Modern historians categorized the style as a National Folk House a "Shotgun" bungalow, one room wide and thirty feet long. It seemed small in her memory, although adequate fifty years ago. Branches overarched onto the roof, shadowing the tiny gabled porch.

One branch stood out, gnarled and black, a survivor of the ages. Hattie instantly knew it was the gallows limb from which her father Rupert was executed. Through the years Oswega's last act played repeatedly in her mind. She could still see her mother running from the porch to the strained rope and hacking away with the knife, as thunderous blasts lifted her body off the ground, depositing it beneath the remains of her father.

Hattie used the Hickory to line up on the outcropping of rock, and despite the reworked landscape, was able to pinpoint the hiding place where she witnessed the double murder and arson. She walked to the place and stared back at the tree. "It's where I hid while they did it."

Randolph and his father stayed with her. "Was this Grandpa Ketchum's work too?"

Hattie squinted. "He was there. With his wagon. But the murderer's name was Ferguson Thatcher, a deputy I believe."

"Thatcher?" Randolph Bigalow paused. "That was Preacher Elston's grandfather, right dad?"

James nodded. "It surely was." The elder Bigalow explained. "Elston was the Minister who ran the Voting Registration Program for this area back in '64."

"Oh dear." Hattie forced herself to ask the question. "What happened to him?"

"They blew up his church office, and him in it."

"Thatcher's own grandson was murdered too?"

Hattie steeled her nerves. More and more she saw the civil rights movement as not a series of skirmishes with die-hard racists but as a slow, real war.

"And Thatcher himself? What became of him?"

"Suicide 1970. Drank himself blind and shot himself through the ear. Left a note and all. Tragic, I reckon. For the family anyway."

In her mind's eye Hattie could see Thatcher standing outside her home challenging Oswega to betray her daughter. Again, she shook the vision away, mumbling.

"Sorry?" James leaned in to hear better.

The old woman started back to the car. "I can't get anywhere makin' shrines out of things that happen to me, James. I got to take out the lesson and move on." Hattie swallowed a rising lump in her throat. "Like right now."

The Lincoln pulled back onto the road. Hattie was breathing easier, but the challenge to her sensibility was still ahead, as they passed a sign reading "Yellow Pine Seniors Residence, 5 miles."

Chapter 29

"Hold on." Pierce held his hand up like a stop sign. "Let's go back to Bobbi Savoy for a minute. You're really saying she committed suicide, indirectly. You know that for a fact?"

Pierce was becoming agitated. "Didn't she have a ton of friends? And a lot to live for, if she'd just cleaned herself up?"

"Friends?" Hattie lifted her gaze to Pierce's quizzical face. "In the drug world?"

"Just listening to that silk voice, the sadness soaked up into those words . . ." Pierce stared at the ceiling with closed eyes.

"Her energy was life, not death. That girl connected with my world and brought me through some terrible times! In my adolescence I felt she knew me, maybe would have loved me."

"Mr. Pierce, Bobbi Savoy loved audiences, but she didn't care much for people."

"What about Lovae?" He sat back. "Didn't she love Lovae?"

Hattie thought about it. "No, not like a mama ought. But she sure wanted to. Lord almighty." Hattie looked away. "I know all about that."

"You know that *how?* You mean Reuben?"

"Of course not! I'm talking about my first baby. The one with no name."

"So you wind up with no family, no support system, and no time to do it over. Ironically, I'm in the same boat. No family. If things went south for me, I'd be bailing with my hands."

"That kind of brings us full circle then Mr. Pierce. My family happens to be the thousands of souls out there that pick up your newspaper and look for answers. The ones who have been burned out, relatives killed, in or out of prison, broke, doped up or going crazy. Mothers losing babies at any age. You know, the ones actually bailing with their hands right now."

"That's fine. But the paper can't cater to the unfortunate exclusively. How about stories of fulfillment, a life rewarded!" Pierce leaned forward. "How about a boy in trouble that got turned around and did something with his life."

Hattie grinned. "Sounds like you know that boy!"

"Just the opposite of a boy who was given every advantage and then got cancelled in a horrible mistake."

"Reuben lives, Mr. Pierce."

"You said that and I'm happy for you. But respectfully, that's a notion in your head, Hattie, no one else's."

"No, I mean he lives on in greater ways Mr. Pierce, partly because of the city."

"The police shot down your innocent son." Pierce was clearly ill at ease. "And I see here they settled with you."

He looked up. "Pardon me Miss Plain, but Reuben was the entire focus of your life, the object of your sacrifice. You gave yourself up for his future." The executive shrugged. "What does a legal settlement do in the face of that?"

"Well, Mr. Pierce." Hattie nodded. "The entire amount, one hundred thousand dollars went right into a scholarship fund for young black men who aspire to journalism as a career. That's what a settlement can do!"

Pierce let the words settle in. "What?"

**

1981

The Lincoln arrived at the Yellow Pine Residence without much conversation among the three passengers. James Bigalow ushered Hattie into the lobby. A passing orderly stopped.

"Afternoon, Mr. Bigalow."

"We've come to visit J.J. Ketchum."

"Yes sir, he might be in the main hall, or try his room."

Hattie followed James Bigalow into 16B. There the old man lay sleeping with an oxygen tube in his nose.

"Grandpa, good afternoon. This is James, and I got a friend with me."

The sleeping Ketchum opened an eye. "Yeah? Who?"

Hattie moved into his view. "Mr. Ketchum I'm Miriam Jones. Do you remember me?"

The old man shook his head. James leaned over and whispered. Then he nodded to Hattie.

"Well Mr. Ketchum, you led a Klan attack against a group of us at the park in 1929. Your wagon killed my Aunt. My father went after you and he was jailed. Do you recall any of this?"

Again, the old man shook his head.

"Mr. Ketchum, you were named in an editorial written by Ponce Davis and me, and distributed to thousands of blacks in this town. Later that day you and your fellow Klan members rode against Mr. Davis. I witnessed that lynching. Do you remember what you did?"

The old man's face remained unexpressive. A moment passed before James spoke. "Respectfully Miss Plain, I think you can see that grandpa does not comprehend much if any of this. I think we should go."

Hattie pressed on. "You and your gangsters followed me home, didn't you? You volunteered your wagon as the gallows. You and Thatcher killed my parents, and burned my house to the ground."

Miss Plain! Please." Bigalow touched her arm.

Hattie pulled away. "He shouldn't die this way, Mr. Bigalow." She looked into the dim eyes of the bedridden old man.

"You a God-damned Knight of the God-damned Ku Klux Klan, Mr. Ketchum, where is your pride? Be courageous enough to stand up for your beliefs. Confess to me right here, right now, that your biggest failure in life is that I'm still alive . . . admit it!"

Bigalow held up his hand. "Please no more. He's not evil. He's just a sick old man."

Hattie shook her finger at the prostrate patient.

"Don't you be braggin' on how much merchandise credit you gave the poor people you helped oppress. The same wagon that delivered goods to the people delivered death to my family!"

Hattie circled him as he followed her with his eyes. "And don't you be hidin' behind an oxygen mask and askin' for mercy from the whole world, like you the victim here. Shame on you! March into hell proudly!"

Bigalow stepped between them. "Alright then, that's it! Time to go."

Ketchum growled. "We hanged the uppity sonofabitch. Shot his whore. Burned them out. Went after the pickaninny too." He looked straight at Hattie. "Too bad we didn't get you."

Hattie felt nausea sweep through her. This closure was why she had come.

"You'll face justice before you face your maker, Mr. Ketchum, if I have say about it!"

The old man bellowed. "I can make one call and you'll never get back to Harlem!"

Bigalow was speechless. "What? Grandpa!"

"Leave us!" The old man waved an arm. Bigalow and Randall exited the room.

Hattie gazed at the old man. "You're a sick, chicken-hearted, cold blooded killer, Mr. Ketchum. But you got something I like."

He coughed and nodded. "What's that, cancer?"

"Honesty. You also run a good bluff."

"And you give as good as you get. Don't scare too easy, I like that. Hell, I like you too."

Hattie poured herself a water. "How'd you know about Harlem?"

The old man relaxed his voice. "I've known you were coming awhile. Didn't know when."

"How?"

"Mitchell over at the Chamber, he came over a few years ago and told me you had been in touch. He told me murder charges were now hanging over my head, and that he would have to inform the sheriff. Well he did, of course the sheriff can't do anything without an eyewitness or confession. So I figured if you were smart, you'd come on down here and file charges. I would if our places were reversed."

"If our places were reversed Mr. Ketchum, you'd be dead."

Ketchum pulled himself up onto the pillow. "Miss Jones, do something for me please."

The name Jones seemed foreign to Hattie, particularly so from this murderer. "Hmmm. Do what?"

"Press murder charges against me. I've written out a full confession to be delivered to the sheriff after I die. But I'll tell the orderly to mail it today to the sheriff. I deserve to die in a real prison with bars on the windows. Beats the hell out of this one."

She took his hand. "I'll sure give it thought, Mr. Ketchum."

"No, no. Don't think about it. Do it! And don't let my family know we were civil to each other today. I can't be a good guy to them, it would be a lie. I got to be remembered for the mean sonofabitch that I was. Maybe my sins will teach them something."

"Well, I'll just be gettin' along now, sir." Hattie opened the door and took a last look.

Ketchum raged on. "And don't let the sun set on your head, hear?"

James Bigalow ushered Hattie down the polished hallway. "I'm sorry, Miss Plain. He doesn't mean it."

"Oh, he's still an old fox. Mr. Bigalow. You know, he wants me to press charges. And I will."

"Good. He earned it. I actually did overhear the whole thing, Miss Plain. He's terribly conflicted, you know. a victim of his upbringing."

Hattie paused at the door. "Really, Mr. Bigalow, how did you escape?"

Bigalow held open the door. "I'll see to it the confession goes to the sheriff."

Hattie Plain felt a rush of success as she exited the front door. "And I'll testify, sir."

Bigalow rubbed his face. "There probably won't be a trial, just an arraignment and a judgment." He turned and examined the low brick facility. "Fifty years later, a man of amazing accomplishment and awful lapses winds up with disgrace and prison as his legacy." He wiped off his forehead with a handkerchief. "Can I take you to your hotel now?

"Yes, I need a few hours alone. Confessions are good aren't they, Mr. Bigalow?"

"I suppose Grandpa Ketchum is going to feel better even if it's for the short remainder of time he has left."

"Oh, I expect it will help him for a good long time after that, Mr. Bigalow."

Hattie Plain returned to the motel and found writing paper in the room. Two hours later she reappeared in the lobby with a sealed letter. She handed it to Julie. "How much postage is it gonna take, girl?"

"Let's see where it's going . . . ah, Nashville Tennessee?"

Julie dropped the letter on her scale. "Three plus ounces. Okay, that's a whole 39 cents."

"When you think that letter is gonna arrive?"

Julie smiled. "Three days max." She looked around for the manager. "Oh remember Mr. Goins has the driver Clarence at your disposal while you're visiting us."

Hattie grinned. "Good then, Clarence can take me to the East Hattiesburg Caller."

The clerk picked up the phone and spoke briefly.

"He's on his way up."

Chapter 30

**

"Let's see now." Hattie stood with her eyes closed, tracing figures in the air with her finger. "Since 1964 this little fund has awarded twenty-five scholarships worth almost a million dollars. And still got almost a million left. Funny how the stock market works."

"And compound interest." Pierce took out his pen. "What is the name of your Fund?"

Hattie closed her eyes, grinning. "The R.B. Handler Journalism Scholarship Award. I donated the original money, but it is entirely independent from me, you know, the thing is handled by a big accounting firm. My only rule is, the panel of judges who interviews candidates must be real working people. I get one report a year."

Pierce looked up from making notes. "You're really the sponsor of the Handler scholarship?

"Yeah the money came to me in a check and the foundation got it all. You know, Mr. Pierce, I got no heirs except Lovae maybe, so I suppose I'll give her my estate when the time comes. All three hundred dollars, depending on the day of the month."

"Excuse me." James Pierce stood and walked to corner of the room. "You're the sole sponsor of the Handler Award?" He rubbed his face. "You're sure?"

Hattie smiled. "You still want to write me a check for ten thousand dollars and send me home?"

Pierce pulled his chair closer. "Miss Plain, let me tell you something about me, okay?"

"Like you said, Mr. Pierce, I show you mine, you show me yours."

Pierce opened his wallet and displayed a family portrait of a soldier and a girl wrapped in a sari. "I was born in 1962. Mother was East Indian; father a black Army sergeant somewhere in the world.

"I grew up with seven siblings outside Kansas City. My father died in Vietnam and mother struggled under the load. Everybody worked except me. I was rudderless, arrested so many times, I was under the supervision of the county courts most of my teen years. I knew cops better than my own siblings."

Hattie nodded. "You was young, see, no sense yet."

Pierce continued. "In 1978 I robbed a store, jacked a car and drove it a hundred miles an hour through town into the next county.

But the police didn't chase me. They followed me and waited till I ran out of gas, then grabbed me when I tried to run. Turns out there was a sleeping baby in the back that I never saw. It wasn't hurt, I argued, what was the big deal?"

Hattie nodded slowly. "It was all just about you back then, wasn't it?"

The executive jumped up and walked around the room. "It took a few weeks for me to get some perspective on this crime and its potential consequences. I began to empathize with the mother, and then her family and then with the community. I thought about my own mother and her sacrifices. For the first time I saw my life as a remodeling job."

"Your mother set the tone then." Hattie grinned.

"Completely!" Pierce was animated. "I started changing things. If it was dirty I cleaned it, broken I repaired it. Family, neighborhood. Parks. Downtown missions, my own church. Reorganized the pressroom at the local paper. I was happy being important to the community! I felt good, better than I hoped."

His voice dropped. "But my mother never saw my change, never knew. She passed on when I was seventeen."

Hattie rocked slightly in her chair, "Oh she knows, baby, she knows all about you."

"The judge eventually assigned me to ride with the gang unit of the police department. He required me to keep a diary and submit it to him every week, and I did. At the end, he asked me to write an essay on who I believed I was, and why I did what I did. And, what I'd learned. I did that too."

"And you just kept writing, didn't you?"

Pierce nodded with enthusiasm. "Writing reveals your own thoughts to you. I discovered when I understood things better, I could change them! Yes, I wrote, non-stop. But 1983 came and I was broke and black with two years of community college, and no real experience. And I wanted to run a newspaper."

Pierce gazed at the wall pictures.

"I needed a formal education. The goal was Columbia University. But the college credits I had wouldn't all transfer, and I sure didn't have any money. I needed help."

"You did, honey, you surely did."

"Thank God I was able to snag a scholarship and within six months I moved to New York and started Columbia, graduated with both a Bachelors and Masters in Journalism then on to Harvard for a business degree. In the next twelve years I was able to do those things I'd dreamt of, able to make changes for the better in three different papers. And now," he looked at her with a knitted brow, "I've taken on this turn-around."

Hattie smiled. "Bigger headache than you thought?"

Pierce waved his arm. "Deeper. The family never developed the right infrastructure or set standards that could be replicated and taught. They drew out the money and failed to reinvest properly. And now they're losing their presence, advertisers are deserting; the writers are shopping their resumes all over the street. And worse, there's no buzz."

"Buzz?"

"People need to be *talking* about you." He punched the air. "Buzz!"

"Well, I'm sure you'll figure out what to do with the *Daily Record*." Hattie checked her watch. "I see our time is up, Mr. Pierce." She pushed herself out of the chair. "Now, are you going to hire me as the Advice columnist, or not?"

Pierce held out a restraining hand. "I'm not done."

"Excuse me." She relaxed again. "I thought we took this all the way home."

"There's two more things and then we're all through. You know, the scholarship I mentioned; well, I had to sit in front of a group of folks that I never expected to see on such a panel. A carpenter, an ex-con running a church, a small newspaper owner, a bookkeeper, a teacher, an unemployed social worker and a garbage collector. We talked about the world, the weather and football. Race relations and fairness. What people go through to get from one month to the next."

"Real things."

"Yeah, real things." The boss waxed enthusiastic. "It was the most extraordinary interview imaginable considering the stakes!"

He turned to her, and she saw the tears standing in his eyes.

"They recommended me for the scholarship, Miss Plain."

"Well, good."

"Your scholarship, of course." He blinked away the tears. "Did you know that before you came down here?"

"Honey, I don't see the list."

"I had no idea you were behind it . . ." Pierce blew his nose. "I just know that without your sacrifice, there's no way the two of us would even be talking tonight." Pierce knelt. "Hattie Plain, Miriam Jones, angel from God, thank you."

Hattie let her own tears of joy run. "You're welcome son. Reuben is proud too."

Pierce put his handkerchief away and arose. "Alright then, last item. What do you want to call the column?"

"'Ask Hattie.'"

"Too fifties. How about 'Hattie on Life?'"

"Too preachy."

Pierce thought. "How about the 'Buzz'?"

She nodded. "Make it 'Plain Buzz'."

"That works!" Pierce grabbed her hand and shook it.

"Start tomorrow. Thousand dollars a week till we see something happen. Let me keep the resume and the essays. They'll be book resources, if you get big."

Pierce picked up the phone and punched three numbers.

"Sykes, get Hattie Plain on payroll, she starts in the morning. I'll email you the details. What? Sykes, I'm not asking you to run references or check her criminal history. She did all that for us. Get her on payroll, now."

Chapter 31

Pierce punched the intercom. "Ricky take Ms. Plain to her home, take care to walk her to the door and wait till she closes it before you leave." He turned to Hattie. "Hattie, please send in Lonnie on your way out."

Hattie squinted at her watch. "Well I see it was ninety minutes exactly, Mr. Pierce. Your agenda is tighter than a frog's hiney, I'm gonna like it fine here."

Hattie turned toward the door as Mallory came in.

"Mr. Pierce, Miss Plain, there's a man here asking for Hattie Plain. Says he's from Hattiesburg, Mississippi. A Vernon Thatcher, I think he said?"

Hattie was puzzled. "Thatcher?" She looked at Pierce. "Can it be?"

Pierce shrugged. "What do you have to lose?" He turned to Mallory. "Let him in. For a minute."

Thatcher walked in slowly, a tall man bent over slightly.

"Folks, I'm Vernon Thatcher. In case you're wondering, I'm eighty-six years old." His white hair fell onto his tall forehead. He was dressed in a blue blazer and gray slacks.

"I happen to be visiting Connecticut, driving cross country. I was watching television in the RV earlier this evening when I saw a report that a woman named Hattie Plain was in some trouble in this building. So, I came right over." He looked at Hattie. "That's you right? AKA Miriam Jones?"

"If I'm Miriam Jones, how do you know me as Hattie Plain?"

"I stay in touch with people in Hattiesburg." He chuckled. "You are not unknown there."

Pierce stood up. "Why have you come here Mr. Thatcher? As you see Hattie Plain is fine."

Hattie strained to study his face. "How do you know me, sir?"

Thatcher leaned on his cane and traded stares with Hattie.

"My father murdered your parents."

Hattie gasped and stared at the confessor, unable to speak.

"Don't believe him Hattie, not yet." Pierce jumped up and circled the old man. "Sir, were you there?"

Hattie tried to let it sink in. "When did it happen? Where? How old were you?"

"Yes, I'm afraid I was there. At the Hickory tree. April, Nineteen twenty-nine, I was ten."

"I sure didn't see no children there that night except me." Pierce opened the door and awaited Thatcher's exit. "I don't know how you got a hold of this background but you're desecrating important history with these rants."

Thatcher remained, looking deeply into Hattie's eyes.

"I was the boy in the tree. I tied off the rope that hanged your father."

"The boy in the tree . . ." Hattie looked at Pierce. "That's somethin' nobody knew."

Thatcher explained. "There was a moon that night. From the tree I saw you hiding behind the brush by the rocks. I saw you run after the shack was set afire."

"But you didn't tell them?"

"No. I got sick to my stomach and fell out of the tree. Broke my arm. I left home a month later and moved in with my older brother in Nashville. I eventually became an attorney and a committed pacifist Miss Plain. Civil Rights was *and* is my cause. I ran a Legal Advocacy Group in Tennessee for many years."

"A what?"

"A group of pro bono lawyers defending the legal rights of poor people."

Hattie smiled sadly. "Did you ever go back home?"

"Only for his funeral in 1970. For my mother's sake." He cleared his throat. "I never spoke with him again after that night."

Pierce looked him over. "What about your mother? You abandon her too?"

"I stayed up with her by letter and pictures. She received them at her sister's house. She followed my father by two months. Natural causes."

"You had children of your own?"

"My son Elston became a minister, my daughter lives in England."

"Your son Elston . . . he was murdered too, wasn't he?"

"The sins of the fathers visited upon the children unto the third and fourth generation. It's a sad day when I have to quote the Bible to explain history."

"Sad day?"

"I am an atheist, Miss Plain. I'll go now, seeing that you're not in any trouble." He stood and turned for the door. Then he looked back at Hattie. "But I have one question for you if you don't object."

"Yes, Mr. Thatcher?"

"Did you ever forgive him?"

The old woman squinted against the light behind his head.

"Mr. Thatcher, God has his job and I got mine."

"Me neither, Miss Jones. Good night."

"Good night, Mr. Thatcher." Hattie watched him cross the foyer. He paused by the elevator, looked back and waved. Then the he disappeared into the car and the doors closed. Pierce reflected on the surprise visit. "What are the odds?"

"I don't know what's goin' on around here Mr. Pierce but it sure doesn't allow much room for the atheism argument."

Pierce stared at the elevator door through the window.

"A strange cap-off to the most unusual ninety minutes of my life."

Sitting once more in the lobby a shaken Hattie waited for Potente to take her to the car. It was a good time to open the remaining birthday card. The envelope was oversized and had no stamp, no postmark. But by its floral border Hattie knew from where it came. He must have delivered it himself early in the morning. She opened it and found herself staring at a linen card. "Happy Birthday Hattie!"

Inside the page bore the colorful image of a tree hand-painted in cloisonné style. It was growing by the side of a river. Birds sat in the branches. A little boy was on the swing, watching a girl climb up the trunk. Hattie opened the card and read a simple inscription, "Your loving witness, Benson."

She slipped the card back into her shopping bag just as Potente came off the elevator. He crossed the marble foyer and held out his hand to her. "Ready, Miss Plain?"

The near-centurion wiped her eyes and replaced the glasses. Then she took his arm. "Ready."

Chapter 32

**

July 1981

The wood-slatted brown industrial park sprawled across several wooded acres on the southwest side of Hattiesburg. The driver Clarence pulled off the highway and found the entrance to the parking lot. He guided the vehicle past endless rows of metal bay doors before finding A-10.

A strip of bushes and flowers marked the unit's entrance. To the left of the door was a short bench with a canister ashtray.

Hattie exited the car, her heart racing. Intellectually she knew the times had changed, this wasn't the same building, and the people inside never knew Ponce Davis. But she was thrilled to read the white, stenciled legend on the glass door, The East Hattiesburg Caller, founded 1865. She hurried into the foyer.

The front office of the Caller was modest and sparse except for the array of framed photographs covering the walls. Her heart leapt when she saw the portrait of Ponce

Davis, large and framed above the archway leading into the pressroom. Under the portrait was inscribed his favorite saying drawn from the Book of James in the New Testament. *Deeds not words*.

Hattie grinned, remembering the time she thought it incomprehensible that a newspaperman would adopt such a slogan.

A teenage girl at the desk looked up and chewed gum through the greeting. "Help you?"

Hattie broke from the Ponce Davis homage and engaged the girl. "What's your name, child?"

"My name? Michele."

"Michele … They didn't give you a last name?"

"Banks."

"Well Michele Banks, I'm Hattie Plain. I used to work here."

"You did?" Her jaws moved faster. "Oh yeah, you're really famous, aren't you?"

Hattie was puzzled. "Your publisher is Ralph Benjamin Waters, right?"

"Yeah … R. B. Waters."

Hattie smiled. "Well, I'm here to see him."

The girl scanned the calendar.

"Do you have an appointment?"

"No, honey, I'm a surprise today."

Michele Banks pressed an intercom button, waited, and then shrugged.

"Not at his desk. Must be in the pressroom. Want me to page him?"

"No. I'll wait, that's fine."

Michele looked up again and forced a smile. Hattie returned the courtesy, unable to avoid making a comparison between this girl and the teenage Miriam Jones, now looming larger in her thoughts.

Michele was a mousy girl with small eyes made large by mascara, pouty lips and honey colored hair, teased into unnatural volume. By contrast, Miriam, as Hattie recalled, was gangly, energetic and spring-loaded. And Miriam had talent. To be fair, maybe Michele had some hidden talent too, albeit hard to spot. The biggest difference seemed to be that Michele didn't really want to be here.

The girl fished through her purse and came up with a pack Of cigarettes. "There's some kind of plaque or something with your name on it in the boardroom." She lit up. "So what did you do that everybody knows you?"

"Miss Banks put that thing out right now. What's wrong with you?"

"Sorry." She snuffed the smoke. "Trying to quit."

Hattie narrowed her eyes. "Honey, quit tryin' and just do it."

"I said I'm sorry."

Hattie looked at her. "So now you know why I'm famous. I tell the truth."

Michele finished with the stack of invoices. "The truth? You mean like smoking and stuff? Other people's business? Is that what makes you so important around here?"

"Michele, I ain't nothing but a janitor in New York

City. The important people around here are the ones who gave their lives so that you and I can be in the newspaper business, see? People like Ponce Davis."

"Uh huh." She stuffed the pack into her purse and slipped the strap onto her shoulder.

Hattie noticed a tattoo on her wrist, reading, "Cotton".

"How long you been working here, Michele?"

She rolled her eyes. "Two months. It's a summer job."

Hattie sighed and walked to the window. "How old are you, honey?"

"I'm seventeen." Michele stood up and stretched. She was a pudgy, full-busted girl. "Break time."

The girl pushed through the door and sat on the bench. Hattie followed. "Let me ask you something Michele. You love this business?"

"It's okay I guess." Michele lit up. Smoke wafted in a slow stream past the black windows.

Hattie stood in the half open door. "What do young people do around here these days beside school and a job"

A breeze rustled Michele's big hair. "Hang out with my friends I guess."

Hattie continued the labored conversation. "Do you write?"

"Do I write? Of course. I'm not a retard."

"I mean, do you write for the paper?" Hattie smiled.

Michele looked at her quizzically. "You mean like articles and stuff? No." She took a long drag and coughed, and spit out her gum inadvertantly. "Damn."

Hattie waited until Michele composed herself. "You don't write letters? Ever write down how you feel?"

"I got friggin D's in English, man. Can't write for crap. I'm gonna be a rock and roll singer anyway. Cotton plays guitar, we're gonna make albums, tour, and party."

"What else you gonna do with your life, honey?"

"Get the hell out of here I suppose." She glanced up at Hattie. "Just forget it."

Hattie sat next to her. "Who you so mad at?"

She jammed the butt into the ashtray. "Nobody, I guess. I don't know. Everything, maybe. I'll be okay when I have the baby." She gazed across the parking lot. "Cotton gets out of the Army next month. Gonna dump his bitch wife, then we're going to Memphis and move in together. There's so many cool clubs and stuff. Cotton is really good on guitar, people like him a lot. And I'll bring the baby to concerts, and it'll be so cool. But he's gonna get a security job at Graceland at first." She exhaled with eyes shut and a smile playing at her lips. "One thing at a time."

"Yeah, baby." Hattie nodded. "That oughtta do it."

"Do what?"

"Take care of the emptiness that's killin' you."

The girl sneered. "You don't know me."

"Why you doin' this to yourself?"

Michele turned, her eyes flashing under the make-up. "Cause I'm so goddam sick and tired of all this crap!"

"What crap, Michele?"

"It's not like I'm famous like you or some actress or whatever. I make minimum wage. I can't even be a hairdresser even though my vocational test scores were really high. My mother's boyfriend who was going to put up the money for school…"

Hattie broke in. "Michele."

The teenager began weeping. "And Cotton loves me, he said so. And the baby will love me. And Cotton will love the baby." She threw the cigarette into the parking lot and held her face. "You people don't know shit."

"Michele."

The girl looked up with tears in her eyes. "What?"

Hattie ran a hand over her shoulder and squatted down to face her flooded eyes.

"I want you to do something nobody else in the world can do, except you. Write the feelings that got stirred up in you, the day you met Miriam Jones. And what you gonna do when your man changes his mind about everything. And what that baby is gonna mean for a single teenage girl with no education. A girl looking for her own voice."

Then Hattie got up and went to the door, turning back briefly to the unhappy teen. "And when you got it all down on paper, read it. Every day for a week. And after that, ask God how you can really become important to this world."

Hattie closed the door.

A middle-aged, light-skinned, black woman waited in the arch until Hattie saw her. She was dressed in a pants suit, and carried a stack of folders in her arms. "Hello, I am Sheila Waters, are you being helped?"

"I'm Hattie Plain, Mrs. Waters."

"You're Hattie Plain?" Sheila stepped back, dropping the folders. "Oh my God. You're actually here…!" Her hands went to her cheeks. "I'll get RB right away. It will be a minute; he's outside with the newsprint people." She gathered files off the carpeted floor and stood again. "You sit now, would you like some coffee?"

"No thank you, Miss Waters, I'll just look at the pictures and pass the time with this wonderful girl Michele."

Sheila Waters disappeared through the arch. Hattie resumed browsing the walls. Before her was something she never expected to see, a scrapbook of her heritage maintained lovingly in a first-class gallery.

She recognized early images of Davis with various notables, and felt thrilled that the pictures had survived nearly seventy years. Oddly, the display although intriguing, didn't move her into a world of melancholy as she feared it would.

Gazing at the ancient scenes, she felt stronger. So much of the past no longer even existed. There were aerial photos of the Negro section of Hattiesburg built along Mobile Street. Now he entire village was just ruins on the riverbank, washed away in the '74 floods.

She pondered old pictures of the Klan assembled in front of the courthouse. The Klan was gone. The notoriously corrupt post-slavery politicians were gone along with most of the tenant-run cotton farms.

Don't make a shrine out of the past. There was plenty to do in the present. The spirit that moved Ponce Davis to a life of service and sacrifice still lived in her heart, and hopefully everywhere within the walls of this building. And maybe in the new Hattiesburg.

That's when her eyes landed on a picture of Davis and his teenage protégé, Miriam Jones herself, standing in front of the Caller's original building. For a moment time disappeared. Hattie stared at the picture, processed the time and place, sorted out the memories that came bundled with it. The gravity of the discovery was overwhelming. She was just thirteen then. The occasion was her joining Davis as a part-time worker. She forbad herself to enshrine her past, she wouldn't worship it, wouldn't weaken under its spell, and finally wouldn't die from it. But this was different. This was original evidence of her promise. The gift. What had she done?

She suddenly felt a wave of fear that she had abandoned the gift. Had run from it. Had her original idealism been crushed? Was the promise squandered?

Michele Banks returned to her desk. "Sorry."

Hattie blinked away the memory and looked at her. "About what, baby?"

"That… I didn't really know you and everything. I'm going to write like you said. And sing."

Hattie grinned. "Get to know what a beautiful and talented person you really are. Find your voice. Then have a baby."

Michele closed an open file. "It's too late."

Ralph Benjamin Waters appeared in the doorway, beaming.

"Miss Plain? Or do you prefer 'Miss Jones'?"

Hattie looked up, and then slowly arose. The middle-aged man was in a short-sleeved shirt with a circular badge pinned to the pocket. It read *Hattie for President*. In the overhead light he resembled Ponce Davis except he was heavier. His wife held on to his arm and smiled from ear to ear. Behind him the employees had assembled, straining for a view of this town heroine.

Hattie broke into a wide smile. "Hattie Plain, Mr. Waters. Just call me Hattie."

Chapter 33

**

Hattie donned her shawl and moved toward the elevator. Suddenly the frantic shouting of a familiar shrill voice reverberated in the opening elevator.

"Hattie!" Ruth's tone was unmistakable.

She charged across the carpet with Johnny Hughes behind.

"Hattie honey, we saw the television. You all right? Johnny brought me down here. What's happening with all these people honey? I got the FBI right behind me. They gonna straighten this out right now. You gonna be all right."

Hattie glanced around. "FBI? Here?"

Behind her, the attorney Thatcher had returned to the lobby and stood by the drinking fountain. Pierce looked over at him.

"Nothing personal, Mr. Thatcher, but we thought you left." Thatcher almost whispered. "The Feds are here Mr. Pierce. It could be an issue with Miss Plain, and I want to be available."

"Dear Lord!" Hattie excused herself and disappeared into the rest room foyer.

A man and woman walked off the elevator behind them.

"Hold it folks. FBI cold case investigators Fordham and Gutierrez. Stay where you are please."

The woman looked through the faces. "Miriam Jones? Please step forward and identify yourself."

Pierce came forward. "I'm James Pierce, Managing Editor. No one here by that name."

"Is someone using an alias, Mr. Pierce?"

Pierce checked his watch. "It's after ten pm for God's sake. You're with Cold Case? And it can't it wait till the morning?"

Gutierrez produced a notebook. "Mr. Pierce, do you employ a Miriam Jones?"

Pierce snapped back. "No, I do not."

The male agent continued. "Do you know her whereabouts at this time?"

Lonnie folder her arms. "I'm Longine Albrecht the owner here. If we don't know Miriam Jones, how would we possibly know where she is?"

The woman agent answered. "She's not at her residence. One of her neighbors seems to think a woman by that description is here tonight. She might be using a different name." She looked around.

Gutierrez checked out the Wal-Mart bag. "She would Probably be in her nineties. Might be carrying around a shopping bag."

He turned to Agent Fordham.

"Roberta, check the restroom."

Lonnie got up. "It's my newspaper, I'll check the restroom."

Thatcher spoke. "Why are you even interested in busting a ninety-year-old woman?"

"Cut the games, folks," he ordered. "Harboring a fugitive is a crime."

Thatcher interrupted him. "She's not a fugitive, Agent Gutierrez. She has not been charged with a crime."

The agent looked up. "Who are you, sir?"

"Vernon Thatcher, attorney at law. My fifty-lawyer firm specializes in civil rights issues. I represent the person you're seeking."

"Mr. Thatcher we recently received a referral from the AG of Tennessee. He had received a hand-written letter dated 1981 from one Miriam Jones in which she confessed to committing two murders near Knoxville in 1929. Says she was interviewed by the Knox County Sheriff at the time, claimed innocence and was released. She proceeded on to New York. The Tennessee Justice Department declined to investigate, but forwarded the confession to us on a hunch."

"When did this confession reach you?"

"A month ago." The agent checked his notes. "Her return address is an apartment on 125th Street. We were out there today. There's no Miriam Jones at that address. But the neighbor here says an old lady answering that description came here today."

He eyed the Wal-Mart bag again.

Lonnie spoke. "I presume you brought the search warrant with you, Mr. Gutierrez."

The agent shrugged. "You make us jump through hoops tonight, and we'll show you a world of hoops tomorrow, Miss Albrecht."

Lonnie's voice rose as she headed for the Ladies Room.

"Your case consists of a confession letter written by an old woman possibly suffering with dementia concerning events that happened seventy-five years ago. Haven't you got some terrorists to chase or something?"

Gutierrez closed the file folder. "I don't choose the caseload folks. We don't want to hurt her; but we have to talk with her. And rest assured, Miss Albrecht, we will do that tonight with or without your cooperation."

A moment of silence went by.

Then Ruth yelled out. "I'm sorry honey, I didn't know you was duckin' the law!"

"You doin' fine, Ruthie." Hattie's voice came from the dark foyer of the restrooms.

Lonnie stepped out of the shadow with Hattie on her arm. She instantly recognized the agents from the morning's visit to 125th Street.

"I am Miriam Jones," said the old woman. "I wrote that letter."

"Miriam Jones, you are under . . ."

"Wait!" Thatcher held up a hand. "I wish to speak with my client."

Hattie looked him over. "Client?"

He ushered Hattie to a corner.

"Miss Plain, I'll explain." The two conferred for a moment.

Thatcher returned to the agents. "She admits to the shooting of two men in self-defense. However, Tennessee has jurisdiction and as you pointed out, has declined to investigate. And she broke no Federal law. So…" He pointed to the elevator. "Good evening, gentlepeople."

Hattie folded her arms. "I was raped by those two men. And they was fixin' to do it again."

Fordham kept her oval face in game mode.

"One of her two victims was a Federal Treasury Agent, Chauncey Jackson, undercover in the Tennessee bootlegging industry. That makes it FBI business, Mr. Thatcher, longstand-ing though it may be."

Pierce jumped in. "Doesn't matter if he was the President. He raped her. She's entitled to defend herself."

Fordham took Hattie's arm. "Miss Plain, you can explain yourself to the US Attorney."

"Stop it right now, please." Thatcher stepped in front of Hattie. "Let's not lose control of this thing. Your man was shot while engaged in the commission of a felony against Miss Jones. She killed him. We break even, agent. Go home."

Gutierrez defended his decision. "My jurisdiction begins and ends with the murder of Mr. Jackson, a Federal Agent. You sir, offer no proof, evidence or witness outside of the subject herself that a crime was underway, or self-defense was at play."

He turned to Hattie Plain. "Miss Hattie Plain aka Miriam Jones, you are under arrest for the murder of Federal Agent Chauncy Jackson on the night of April 15,

1929 in the county of Knox, Tennessee. We will forgo the placement of wrist restraints. Miss Plain, would you like a wheelchair?"

Hattie stood by the chair where she had spent most of the day. Her advice to Bobbi seventy-five years earlier now rang hollow, hasty and plainly untrue.

Girl has to change her name if she's going to the top. Or her past might reach out and hold her back.

She leaned on the cane and let out a trembling sigh. "I don't want nothing from you." Her eyes filled and overflowed. "You know, I been hired twice in my life to work full-time as a writer for a real newspaper. Seems like both times it was a short career."

She gave each of her new colleagues a final look. "I thank you all for your consideration. Especially you Mr. Pierce." She turned quickly to avoid their stricken faces. "Take care of my resume, Ruthie," she said. "It's all I got."

Agent Fordham shook off the moment and handed Lonnie Albrecht a card. "This is how to reach me. In fact," she scribbled a note on the back, "My cell number. I don't give that out to the public. But this is a special case, she is ninety-two." Fordham gave up a grin. "Who knows."

The elevator doors opened. Hattie and the agents boarded and were gone.

"Lord almighty, I gave up my best friend to the police." Ruthie went to the elevator. "Hattie I'm gonna help you, "she yelled. "I'm comin, honey!"

Pierce shot a look of distain at Thatcher. "Well, go help your client, Mr. Thatcher!"

"I can't." The white-haired man upturned his palms. "I'm not licensed to practice in New York, just Tennessee."

Pierce reacted. "You were bluffing the FBI?"

Ruth went to the Wal-Mart bag. "Well, I'll make sure she gets her diary back!"

"Her what?" Thatcher looked up and stayed Ruthie's hand. "Did you say *diary?*"

Ruthie answered. "Ain't that what it is? A diary? Of her whole life?"

Pierce chimed in. "She and I just went through it!"

Thatcher pulled the books from the shopping bag. "Anything that addresses this rape and shooting episode?"

Pierce nodded. "Oh yeah. There's a ton. And she can spin it!"

Lonnie asked, "Is it helpful?"

"It's honest!" The editor laughed.

Thatcher looked up at Lonnie. "Miss Albrecht you have the agent's cell number, right? Call it. Don't let them get back to the shop, it'll be too late, they'll put her in the system. Get them back up here!"

Lonnie fished for her phone. "What is it we have?"

"A *diary.* Ruth just nailed it. A diary is evidence in court." He turned and smiled ear to ear. "We have a witness!"

Chapter 34

"White Slavery!" Thatcher chuckled at the irony as he hauled out the thick notebooks.

"Heard of it." Lonnie pulled the business card from her pocket card and began dialing. "What exactly was that?"

"The Mann Act passed in 1903. Known as the White Slavery Act." Thatcher leafed through the pages. "Makes it a crime for an adult to transport a minor across a state border for immoral purposes."

Lonnie got Fordham on the line. "Please return, Miss Fordham. Now! Miriam Jones committed no crime. Your arrest is invalid. Your man was a criminal. We have a witness!"

Lonnie hang up and turned to the others. She was upbeat.

"Well they're coming back. Not real happy though, I think."

Pierce glanced at the elevator lights. "We'd best find something fast, folks."

Mallory, Johnny Hughes, Lonnie, Potente, Pierce, and Thatcher split the essays up and began poring through them.

Mallory scanned an early journal. "Can't find any reference To a rape," she griped.

"Try looking for a train ride," admonished Pierce.

Moments later the elevator doors opened, and the agents helped Hattie back onto the foyer floor. Gutierrez saw the huddle.

"Let's get something straight, Mr. Thatcher. You better make this good. You say you have a witness, show me."

Thatcher took Hattie's arm and guided her to the corner.

"Whatever you have in the bag about the train to Knoxville, dig it out." He narrowed his eyes. "Everything! Now!"

Hattie went to the bag and withdrew the correct essay. Her hand shook as she handed it to Thatcher.

**

April 15 1929. The northern part of Mississippi is different from the Hattiesburg area. I stay glued to the window except for writing these Essays on Life, although there's no newspaper left to print them. My sadness has been noticed by a fellow traveler.

The train clacked along the Dixie route north through Mississippi toward Knoxville where Miriam would make connections to Georgia, then New York City. She had cried most of the day and finally fallen asleep. She awoke to find a large man seated next to her.

"Say girl, you travelin all by yourself?" The moon-faced man smiled and looked her over. Miriam had never seen any man in a plaid suit, spats, and a Bowler hat.

"Me and my uncle," she lied. "He's a lawman, rides in the caboose. Carries a gun."

"You don't say. Well my name's Price. Vernon Price. Doctor Vernon Price." He flashed a metal badge. "Workin' for the railroad right now, special assignment."

"Hattie Plain." Miriam could hardly get the unfamiliar words out. Cautiously she shook hands with her fellow traveler.

"Look here girl, I've got a powerful hunger comin on, and I see the train is stopping here at Knoxville this evening. Now there's a diner just outside town serves up the finest fried chicken in Tennessee. Bring your uncle and it'll be just like down home Sunday dinner, yes ma'am. Just a half-mile outside the station."

Hattie pointed to her suitcase. "I got me a dinner right here."

"Say, you ever drive around in an automobile?"

"No sir, I sure haven't."

"Well that's another reason for you to come along. My cousin got himself a new Buick, yes indeed. And he's a government man, you know. Goes after the people makin' booze, heh heh. Why, he'll pick us up and we'll drive on out there just as fancy as you please and have us a dinner so good you be talking about it to your grandchildren!"

"That's generous sir, but I got me a meal right here all ready to eat and I don't have to move ten feet except for the rest room."

Hattie opened a wax paper package and found it empty. The short bread cookies had disintegrated into crumbs and spilled out into the suitcase.

"Look here, we just go on out there and eat, let your uncle sleep. I'm buying, you know. You ain't gonna have to spend a penny, no ma'am, not one penny."

Hattie's hunger won out. "Well I suppose . . ."

The train pulled in the Knoxville Station at five pm. Hattie carried her own bag. Vernon Price stayed close by her side. They walked away from the station onto a dirt road. Price checked his watch. A Sheriff deputy followed them from the platform and spoke, his hand resting on his weapon.

"You folks passing through?"

Price stepped forward. "Sheriff, I was just looking for you. My daughter and I trying to get to the AME Church here in Knoxville. I myself am giving a talk there Sunday. Love Your Neighbor, white or colored, yes sir. Halleluiah."

The deputy looked Price up and down. "AME Church? South side probably."

He ran his hand down the heavy man's suitcoat. "Here's some advice Reverend fancy-pants; spend some money on that girl of yours. Don't look right she's in rags and you in that suit."

"Yes sir and that's what's gonna happen. My exact plan. Thank you, Sheriff."

The pair walked out to the highway and stood at the intersection.

Hattie frowned. "Why did you tell the sheriff I'm your daughter?"

Price looked her over with a scowl. "Cause I'm your daddy."

"Hold up now." Hattie set down her suitcase. "I thought you were a doctor. You're a minister?"

"I'm whatever this world is looking for, honey bunch. I'm doin' fine."

Hattie was about to run for the train when Price took her by the shoulder to avoid a black shiny car pulling up behind them. The driver was a thin man in baggy clothes.

Price helped Hattie in the back seat and shut the door. Hattie was amazed; she had only seen cars from a distance, and nothing this fine "You late, nigga." Price was fuming. "Had me a fine talk with the Sheriff cause you ain't nowhere to be found."

The driver shrugged. "Flat tire, Henry. But I changed it. All good now."

Hattie turned. "Your name's Henry?"

The big man smiled. "Middle name. Vernon Henry Price. My cousin Chauncey Jackson here calls me Henry. Chauncey is a government man."

"Shut up, Henry."

The car pulled off the road at a roadside restaurant. Muffled sounds of music drifted through the night air. The parking lot bordered a tree line. Sounds of a rushing river could be heard deep into the woods. Price and his cousin took Hattie through the front door. There was a loud band and lots of odd-looking dancing. The smell of alcohol was in the air. Women in their underwear paraded with trays of drinks.

Hattie stopped. "There's no fried chicken here, Mr. Price. I think we need to go."

Price was busy kissing one of the girls. Chauncey pulled Hattie into a corner booth. "We'll let Henry say hello to his friends. Hasn't seen them in a few years."

"Where's he been?"

"Where's he been?" Chauncey stared at her for a minute, then laughed. "You ain't working for him?"

"No sir, he's just a man I met on the train."

"Prison for ten years, girl." Chauncey ran his hand over Hattie's suitcase and up across her chest, whispering, "You know, I got me a special gift. I can smell true love a mile away."

He patted Hattie's breasts and smiled. "Right there in your heart, ain't it?"

Hattie clutched the luggage with crossed arms.

He cuddled in her cheek. "Say girl, let's have us a little fun of our own."

Hattie was wedged into the corner table. "I got no love for you, sir."

With one hand Chauncey unzipped himself and moved the other hand under Hattie's hem and straight into her crotch. She yelped in pain and struck him in the eye. He grabbed her by the hair and forced her head down toward his lap.

Hattie allowed herself to be pulled down, and then went limp, slipping easily under the table, her suitcase in tow. She crawled out to the dance floor then ran for the front door. Outside she had few options. The road or the tree line. She u-turned and raced for the woods.

Minutes passed. She rested near the river. Clearly her abductors had given up on her. In a clearing under the moon-light, she opened her suitcase and removed the purse with the few remaining dollars. They could have the money if another showdown came. But the photograph and clothes were hers. And her personal dignity. The images of her mother and father wracked her. She turned and threw up on the tree.

"They put back doors on these places for a reason, girl."

Henry's deep voice was behind her. "Now you've gone and messed things up for yourself." He grabbed her by the hair and jerked her head back. "Chauncey tells me you're a little tease. Man can't have any fun that way."

He wiped her nauseous mouth with a handkerchief. "Good as new, baby."

Chauncey kicked the bag, and the purse spilled out.

"Got some money right here, Henry. Room's all ready."

"Mighty fine!" Henry motioned toward the back of the building. "We'll let our new friend here get some reclining rest."

The two men laughed and walked Hattie to the building. They dragged her up the stairs and opened a rear door of a dingy, smelly room. A weak light bulb hung from a cord. Hattie was thrown to the cot. She bounced up and swung at Henry, connecting with his jowl. His yelp was the last thing she heard, as a blow to her head brought darkness.

**

James Pierce laid down the essay and looked around. "Well, there's assault, battery and rape. Intent from the get-go. How about it Agent?"

"Promising but far from clear, Mr. Pierce."

Thatcher spoke. "It's clear the conspiracy began on the train in northern Mississippi, when this man Henry tells her he has an accomplice waiting in Knoxville. He knew there was no chicken dinner; he knew what he's going to do with her. He's about to violate the Mann Act. Does that put the real problem in your jurisdiction?"

"Keep going. Get to the part where she pulls the trigger."

"Miss Plain, what happened then?"

Hattie grimaced. "When I woke up, I felt rather a peculiar pain in my private area, and had a pretty good idea what must of happened. Of course, the money was gone. Well I found the river and cleaned me up, and washed the head wound under a full moon. My other clothes were dirty and bloody, so I unpacked the blue dress." Hattie lowered her voice to almost a whisper. "And don't you know, wrapped up in that dress was a 32 caliber handgun. I lifted it up into the moonlight and saw the cylinder was full of bullets. My Uncle Malcom had thought of everything!"

Chapter 35

April 15, 1929 10pm

Hattie climbed the rickety wooden staircase. The back door to the club was unlocked. She walked in and made her way through the revelers. The music hurt her ears. It took a few minutes to find Henry and Chauncey. Hattie stood where they could see her, then smiled and showed off the dress.

Henry broke off with his lady friend and focused on the teenager.

"Lookie here now, the devil in a blue dress! More, baby? You want old Henry again?"

Chauncey stumbled up and ran his hand over her dress. "Fresh and sweet ain't it Henry?"

Two other men surrounded her. "This is fine looking young, Henry. You sharin' with your friends tonight?"

Henry beamed. "You got five dollars Travis, I got the goods."

The other man tapped Henry on the arm and handed him five.

"Yeah, well I'm in too, brother."

The four men and Hattie walked out the back door to the disdain and hoots of the working girls. The men turned toward the outside private door but Hattie said no.

"I want it by the river," she said coyly.

The walk to the water was hilarious to the four drunks who stumbled and fell constantly. Then an open area appeared in the moonlight next to the rushing water, with a blanket laid out. Hattie told the men to line up, and strip off their trousers. Laughing, they disrobed, arguing about who would be first.

Hattie sunk to her knees and pulled the nickel-plated .32 handgun from a folded blouse. Slowly she brought up the weapon and, controlling the shaking, clicked back the hammer.

"First man moves is gonna bleed."

**

Hattie realized the entire room was hanging on every word. She rolled her eyes.

"I never in my life thought I'd shoot those men. I wanted them to jump in the river and let nature do the job. Oh I knew about guns, you know. Hunted rabbits, squirrel and birds with my daddy all the time. But this was different. These men were vicious criminals who had wronged me something fierce and I had the power to put them out of business. My daddy's instructions ran through my head, just like we was huntin', 'just squeeze the trigger, girl, slow and steady.'"

Gutierrez sighed. "She called them together for the purpose of threatening them. Now who's the conspirator?"

Thatcher held firm. "That's Tennessee's problem, according to what you stated earlier."

"Not when it involves threatening the life of a Federal Agent."

Lonnie squatted next to the old woman. "Hattie, go on."

**

10:20pm

The half-naked quartet tried to sober up quickly, but it was too late. Each man stood out clearly in the moonlight.

Suddenly Henry ran at her but stopped when a bullet slammed through his chest. The thunder clap from the pistol was deafening. Chauncey turned to run but stopped when he saw the gun muzzle pointed at his head.

"I'm with the government!" he yelled. "Don't shoot me."

The teenager held out a hand. "Where is your identification?

"Here!" He fished his wallet out and placed it in the girl's hand as she remained in a shooting posture.

She read it in the moonlight. "You supposed to be six foot five and three hundred pounds. You nothing but a shrimp."

"I lost weight, there was a mistake by the clerk."

"You stole this wallet, didn't you?"

"I found it and that's the truth!"

"And you lyin' like a sheet." Hattie pulled back the hammer with both hands on the weapon. "Where'd you get that car?"

"Okay, I borrowed it from Chauncey. But he's fine and knows all about it." The imposter reached for her hand. "Help me up girl. I'll show you bootlegging money you ain't never seen! And the car, why you can have the car. It's a government car, got the extra speed you know." He got closer. "Please." Then he lunged at her, but Hattie jumped back and fired a round.

The skinny man spun backwards and fell. She shot each of her attackers twice more, then ordered the two other men to dump the bodies in the river. They did. Then she ordered them into the river. They complied and were swiftly carried downstream by the rushing current. Hattie fired at them till the gun was empty, then threw it into the river.

**

Hattie relived the moment with distaste. "I collapsed to my knees and gagged again and again. Time was not on my side. Two of my rapists were dead but the people in the club might become curious at the sound of shots fired. Well I recovered, and saw the pants were all in a heap. I went through all the wallets and pockets. I transferred the stolen money back to my purse and left the car keys for the sheriff."

Gutierrez looked at Fordham and nodded. "The diary is compelling Ms. Plain, but the case is still very much open." He withdrew the cell phone from his pocket and stepped away. "Excuse me."

Hattie closed her eyes, drained from the testimony, oblivious to the excited chatter of her new colleagues. Rehearsing that devastating night in Tennessee left her empty. What if there had been a witness who would have given her up to the sheriff? What if the sheriff was a Klansman who had been alerted to watch for her? What would have been her fate in a Tennessee courtroom, with no family or friends there to assist in the defense?

There was no point in wondering how she'd survive a life sentence in prison. Tennessee was a death state. She would have hanged on her twenty-first birthday. If she survived that long.

So what had life delivered instead? Sixty-one years a charwoman, a victim, a murderer, a whore, a drug addict, mother of two dead children, no man and a future in prison.

Why had fate spared her in Tennessee, only to bring it to this? Now she faced it all over again. Arrest and trial. She would have to be her own witness. Would there be justice?

She thought of Ponce Davis, how he held up the Bill of Rights to a murderous mob, and asked if they understood its meaning. She found herself connecting to that word, *understand*. Different from *accepting*. Freedom of the press meant freedom to publish. Freedom from fear meant freedom from death. Mr. Davis stood for principle. He stood for truth, for things eternal. Suddenly she understood her mentor better.

Davis had been training her from the beginning. He implored her to *carry on*, his very words. Hattie felt the rush. You got to stand. It doesn't matter what happens after that. *Stand*.

"Stand up Hattie!" Ruthie shook her lightly. "Hattie honey, this FBI man is coming up the elevator. You got to be awake, now."

Hattie opened an eye. "You got no idea how awake I am."

Again the musical doors opened and Gutierrez stepped out. He immediately conferred with Agent Fordham. Then he faced the lawyer.

"Mr. Thatcher, we have a lot of lawlessness on both sides in Ms. Plain's account. She undoubtedly killed two alcohol distributors that Agent Chauncey Jackson was investigating but that's Tennessee's case, not ours. The diary convinces us the skinny distributor killed Agent Jackson and stole his wallet and car. Government justice can't be served by arresting your client."

Thatcher nodded. "Does she get a medal for finishing the government's work in 1929?"

"Actually, Mr. Thatcher, your client had no idea who those men were."

Lonnie spoke. "She knew they were rapists, agent."

"We'll save the medal." Gutierrez waited for the elevator car to arrive. "Good night, Miss Plain, folks. Sorry for the interruption."

The door opened and closed, leaving the group standing in half-light. Thatcher seemed lost in thought for a moment.

"Hattie, when did you send that confession to the Tennessee AG?"

Hattie was proud. "Nineteen-eighty-one during my trip to Hattiesburg. I figured if J.J. Ketchum could make a full confession, I could."

Potente seemed lost in thought. "Why would Tennessee wait twenty-four years to act on it?"

Pierce responded. "Could be because a national criminal database was just implemented. Ties unsolved crimes to subjects in the database. Fingerprints, personal data, even DNA. All kinds of matches coming up. Hattie, apparently you were in there I'm sorry to say."

"That's all right, son." She flashed a wide grin. "It's always the right time for real justice."

Chapter 36

One year later

Everett Washington stuck his head in the Security door.

"Hey Potente. You up for some overtime this weekend? Got to reconfigure the security system."

"Again boss? Didn't we just upgrade six months ago?"

"We're bringing in all the operations people. Every support system has to be recalibrated. Phones, codes, passwords, door locks, plumbing." He laughed. "Too much expansion, too quick!"

Potente appeared in the door in civilian clothes. "Wish I could, but I help out my great grandmother on Saturdays. She's got a scarf boutique in the city now. She's taking over the neighboring bay and I'm doing the build-out."

James Pierce walked through with a handful of papers. "Scarf business must be good, Potente."

"Three hundred pieces a week!" The Security specialist spoke passionately. "And she has a new line of bags and hats coming in from Puerto Rico, Mr. Pierce. Nice stuff too."

"Sounds like I'm in the wrong business!" Pierce spotted Lonnie crossing the hall. "Lady A, I need to see you in the morning, eight sharp. Good?"

Lonnie checked her planner. "Straight up." She smiled.

"Hey people, we snagged ten thousand new subscriptions in the past year, half of them out of state. Plain Buzz is the reason. If Hattie does another Oprah, it'll double again in the next twelve months."

Whitefield breathed deeply. "Ah, the energy in this place! Have you ever seen anything like it? What a difference!"

"A year ago, we couldn't get arrested, now we're the talk of the town." Lonnie looked down the hall. "That stubborn, beautiful, crafty old woman is the reason too. She had to force-feed us the formula to success. Why didn't we know?"

"I ain't never seen anybody like that woman." Everett Washington chuckled. "Not that she likes me one bit. I was the one told her to get out before she got herself hurt."

Whitefield protested quickly. "She admires you Everett, it's me she doesn't like. I told her nobody over fifty had a future." Whitefield rolled her eyes. "Imagine saying that to Hattie Plain?"

Lonnie pursed her lips. "Actually, it's me she hates. Ever since that day she single-handedly invaded us. I was paranoid and losing control and I was a monster to her and everyone else. But I tried to make it up." She dabbed her eyes.

Whitefield objected. "Oh, Hattie appreciates you, Lonnie. Me, I tried so hard to purge myself of everything human when I came to work here. Nothing but pandering, compromise and struggle. Then Hattie came. The work is still hard but somehow more fun to do. And I think I'm more forgiving. Aren't you Ev?"

"More tolerant of mistakes maybe." Washington growled. "But I'll bust slackers in ten seconds, that hasn't changed."

Darryl Sykes spoke up. "Whatever it is, it works. Two more Times staff writers are coming in for interviews this week"

Potente raised his coffee mug. "To 'Plain Buzz.'"

The others returned the salute. "The Buzz!"

"Listen up!" Lonnie turned serious. "There's a report circulating that you'll all see sooner or later. So, I'll get in front of it right now. The report says my family was in negotiations to sell this paper but backed out after Hattie was hired." The woman sat on the corner of a desk. She measured her words. "It's partly true."

"Hang on a second, Lonnie." Potente scratched his head. "I asked you if you were trying to sell, and you said..."

"I never denied it, Ricky. You see, we were failing rapidly. It would have been industry knowledge in short time. We had to act. To our surprise the offer was firming up better than anyone thought. We figured, well I figured, it was our last good shot at getting something for the Record. It was headed for bankruptcy.

"In fact, I was on my way to meet with the buyers over dinner, when Hattie showed up and began the whole drama. I called the buyers to say I'd be late. They were suspicious, and off-put to say the least. They apparently heard the news stories about an elderly woman being held and beaten or whatever. Anyway, their lawyer called the next morning and told us the deal was gone." Lonnie smiled. "Thank God. "

Washington chuckled. "So, we're all here today because Hattie Plain intervened."

"Yes. But remember this." Lonnie stood up. "I was acting in behalf of the shareholders. It was, and is, my job description. If I'd simply allowed the paper to go under, you'd all be equally unemployed. By the way, I took the paper off the block that night. "

Potente bit his lip. "Well I guess it's my turn. Lonnie, you've always felt that Mat Perez was part of a conspiracy to blackmail you that night by emailing out compromising photos of Hattie under assault, right?"

Lonnie thought for a moment. "Yes. You told me Benson Ridges of the New York Times had received the pictures and were threatening to publish them! And yes, I took it very seriously."

Potente stood up. "Well I lied. Mat's camera didn't work that way. No photos were ever sent."

Lonnie was stunned. "Why did you lie to me? At such a sensitive moment? On such a huge issue?"

"Because we were wrong, and she was right about nearly everything. And I knew it in my gut. I had a decision to make that moment. You yourself told Breen to make a choice between being a jerk and being a man. I made mine on the spot. I'm not sorry—but I do realize I can't be here anymore."

Lonnie sighed and smiled. "Don't go anywhere, Ricky. We need you right here."

There was a silence for a few moments as each person replayed the events of a year earlier. Finally, Sykes broke the quiet. "You see where Jamie Workman was named editor of the features section at the Times?"

Elizabeth nodded. "Replaced old Benson Ridges. Passed on two days ago. What a legend he was!"

Washington smiled. "The oldest working executive in the newspaper business. Eighty-six, expired on the job."

Lonnie looked at Elizabeth. "Do we know any more about the nature of the decades-long relationship between Ridges and Hattie Plain?"

Elizabeth spoke quietly. "Well what I hear is, Hattie's got it all in her notes, her unpublished articles and letters all locked up in Mr. Pierce's safe, and one day she's gonna publish the whole thing." She raised her voice. "Then we're gonna know all the details about what happened to this charwoman while she cleaned toilets for sixty-one years before deciding to change our whole world."

Hudson entered the room waving a printed page.

"Lonnie, something strange is going on. We just got an email from Benson Ridges at the Times."

Washington smiled. "That's hard to do, Hudson, he's dead."

"I know, I know. It got delayed by two days, apparently our servers stopped it from going through. Had to be hand routed because, well frankly it's coming from a competitor."

Washington looked quizzically. "Two days? My God, it must have been close to the last thing he wrote!"

Lonnie peered at the document. "Who's it addressed to?"

"Hattie." Earl Hudson lowered his voice. "It's personal, I'm sure."

Lonnie broke in. "This is a public communications platform, no one has a right to the expectation of privacy." She held out her hand. "Let's see it."

Chapter 37

Hattie, the hour marking my shuffle from this mortal coil is fast falling, and I choose this moment to reflect a bit (at your expense I'm afraid), as I have no one else to talk to now. And I don't have the gumption to tell you in person what I can better write down on this judgment-free screen.

Well, you and I never got together did we? Sixty years of chances came and went; I guess it wasn't supposed to be, at least not in this round. Truth is, I am a seasoned coward that way.

Did I ever tell you I started with the Times at age seventeen? That was about seventy years ago! You know I did every job at this newspaper except clean the bathrooms and hallways. So I guess you could say between us we did it all.

It isn't well known but my paternal great-grandfather was a silent stakeholder in the original New York Times Company, that's the main reason I stuck around so long. It was job insurance for sure, but it also enabled me to extend a modicum of protection towards the one I came to love.

Also, not well known, my maternal great-grandmother was a Cherokee Indian, and her father was a freed slave. I've borne a slight sadness throughout my life that the family color scheme wasn't more widely revealed, and that I too had facilitated a mute conspiracy to maintain ancestral secrets. There were other ways I didn't fit in so well too, Hattie. I never married of course. But I considered myself lucky to have found someone in this journey whose radiance blinded me, whose courage inspired me and whose soulful gravity simply owned me. That someone is you.

Hattie you found me when bullies were wailing on me, remember? I was twelve, you were a goddess. I ran and sat in the LaSalle and watched you handle that phony chauffer. Oh, how I wanted to take you home with me. Then I found you again working for my newspaper! I looked in on you a hundred times. I drank in your courage, honesty, creativity and intelligence and it sustained me in this alien world. I became a better human being because I found it so easy to love you so much. It didn't even matter whether that love was returned. Without you to gaze upon at least once a day these past sixty odd years, I would have faded into these drab picture-lined walls.

Your struggle for civil rights wasn't just about voting or a place on the bus, it defined moral courage. You put it on the line, while I hid out. You cleaned my building while I edited the crossword puzzle. I made money, you made history.

Please know that your turning down my frail attempt to win you, and your choosing a more difficult way of earning your child's college money, was, I know, not easy for you. We all did what we did; there wasn't as much choice to it as other people would like to think. I hope to see you again soon, not on my terms, but on yours and by the providential grace that brought you to this otherwise lifeless life.

In the meantime, you are unexpectedly now the owner of a small slice of the New York Times. Lawyers will contact you. Want a tip? Sell it back to them. Eternal Love, Benson.

Chapter 38

**

Twelve Years Later

The small cemetery behind Zion Redeemer church accommodated the band of six guests. They stood silently at a gravesite where a hand-carved wooden cross was firmly anchored against a marble shrine bearing the image of a blossoming tree carved in relief.

A soft wind blew off the East River. Whitefield faced the sudden breeze. "Hattie's here."

Sykes looked around. "Don't we wish."

Lonnie Albrecht spoke. "Well I'd love to say something profound, but you know I feel empty. Two hours of eulogies, kind of said it all. Funny though, no tears from me."

Everett Washington agreed. "Me neither. She didn't want nobody getting all weepy anyway, said she'd just be getting on to the next bus."

Darryl Sykes stared at the engraving on the stone. "She was almost a hundred and four. There's a time for each of us I guess."

Washington grunted. "When the job is done."

Hudson examined the wooden cross. "What's the story on that cross? Was Hattie really that religious?"

Lonnie shrugged. "I think she was a Baptist. Wasn't she? Gave herself to Jesus?"

Elizabeth chimed in. "Umm I'm pretty sure she was Catholic. She loved the Pope."

Washington laughed. "Hattie a Catholic? Naw. Hattie was a Christian Scientist. Didn't accept evil as a creation of God, therefore it didn't really exist."

Sykes mused. "I always thought she was a Mormon the way she loved family."

Whitefield ran her hand over the varnished surface of the cross. "So then, where'd this nice cross come from?"

"Well I'll tell you." James Pierce stooped down and drew a diagram in the dirt. "There's a plot of land down in Palmers Crossing Mississippi, part of Hattiesburg. There's a little store on it now, but a hundred years ago it was the home of Miriam Jones and her family. On the southeast corner of the property, right here . . ." he made a cross in the dust, "stood a Witness Tree, a Hickory, planted by the grandmother about 1840 to mark the property line."

"A hickory?" Whitefield thought. "She grew a hickory right there on 125th Street…"

Pierce continued. "Anyway, I went down there recently and found it with the help of a fine man named Randy Bigalow. Fire had scarred the old dame. Lightning had split it. A few branches were no good anymore. But the tree was still there, still standing. So I bought it. Took it down and had a carpenter make up that cross." He looked around. "A witness tree."

"Oh yes, and what a witness she still is!" Whitefield dabbed her eye. "She bought her apartment building and gave the gift of home to others. Started new scholarships, women's counseling centers, just gave it all away."

"Invested it," Lonnie corrected. "Which is a perfect lead-in to the last feature of our Hattie service." She produced a sheet of paper. "Elizabeth and I have put together a scrapbook of some of Hattie's columns, it will be on permanent display in the lobby. I took the liberty of bringing with me her final column published on her birthday last month, which I'd like to read out loud before we go back to work."

> *Dear Hattie: I've been reading your column for years and wouldn't miss it. But I think you're wrong on something you said to Bewildered last month. You said, "Shoot the hostage. honey." Hattie, there's times people threaten something that's precious to you, just to make you do what they want. That's their power over you; it's just how human beings work. You can't let them destroy the "hostage", it may be just too important! Can't we say, "Negotiate the peace?" Signed, Gun-to-the-Head Greta.*

Dear Greta,

Yours is the last letter I'll ever answer in this column, because I'm on to other work, so listen up good. You came in with nothing except a mind ready for life. It's a sure bet you leaving with nothing but a mind full of lessons which are supposed to serve you well later on. Are you going to compromise with evil? Is that what you're teaching yourself to do? How about your children? What are you going to stand for, if you don't stand for what's right? You think it matters what goods may get hurt or what feelings may suffer, if you getting straight with your God? Life is long honey; a lot longer than you may think. Teach yourself to grow straight up and you'll be helping more people than you'll ever know. The children will climb in you and the birds will find a home in you, and you'll stand as a witness to good forever. I love you all, now, go love each other.

Hattie.

The group passed around a box of Kleenex, then headed for the limo. There was nothing more to do or say at the cemetery, but as each one now knew, as each had just been reminded, there was plenty of work ahead.

The End

Made in the USA
Monee, IL
19 July 2023

39580527R00152